CHAPTER ONE

Extensive research has shown that, just like stolen cars that are chopped up and sold in pieces, the human body is worth considerably less than the sum of its parts.

The woman on the television screen didn't look like she was long out of school, and the topic she was discussing was distinctly at odds with her cheery demeanour.

"Do we have to watch this?" Detective Sergeant Erica Whitton said.

"I think it's fascinating," Lucy, her adopted daughter commented.

"Me too," Detective Sergeant Jason Smith agreed. "I didn't know how lucrative human body parts could be."

An investigation into the so-called cadaver scandals has yielded disturbing results, the pretty presenter carried on. *Whereas in the past the illegal sale of body parts was limited to medical schools and research facilities, nowadays the market has grown to include traditional medicines and even cosmetic companies. A 2019 survey estimated the market in human body parts to be worth somewhere in the region of 50 billion dollars worldwide.*

"Can we please turn this off?" Whitton said.

"It's almost finished," Lucy said.

"I can think of more pleasant Sunday evening viewing options," Whitton said. "Human body part trafficking is hardly light entertainment."

"What time is Darren getting back?" Smith changed the subject.

"He shouldn't be late," Lucy said. "He wanted to catch up a bit with his mum and dad."

"Are you sure Andrew will be alright with Darren's parents?" Smith said. Andrew was Lucy and Darren's one-year-old baby.

"They're his grandparents," Lucy said. "They don't get to spend much time with him."

"For the whole week?"

"They know how to take care of a baby. That's really disgusting."

She nodded to the TV screen. The documentary on human body part trafficking wasn't holding back. On the screen was a row of metal tables displaying various organs, limbs and other body parts. The camera zoomed in to show the labels attached to the individual items. Written on each label was an estimation of how much each part was worth on the black market.

"Looks like big business," Smith said.

"I can't believe stuff like that still goes on these days," Whitton said. "It's like something out of the Dark Ages."

"I'm just glad we don't have to deal with human body part trafficking," Smith said.

He didn't know then how wrong he was. In a workshop a few miles away, an unfortunate soul was about to be dissected, and the sum of her parts would soon come to the attention of Smith and the men and women on his team.

CHAPTER TWO

Dr Valerie Kyle scanned the lecture hall and estimated that at least half of the seats were occupied. As Monday mornings went, the turnout wasn't half bad. It was just after nine and a few latecomers were making their way inside. Valerie decided to wait a few more minutes before she began.

The hall was full of low murmuring. The students who'd opted to take the special Anthropology module were no doubt discussing their weekend exploits. Valerie couldn't hear what they were talking about, but if she was privy to one particular conversation she would be shocked by the subject matter. Two women were engaged in a quiet debate about a rumour that had recently surfaced. An urban legend had sprung up about some kind of workshop operating in the city. This was no ordinary workshop – the word on the street was it was a place where human bodies were brought in, in the dead of night. These cadavers were then dissected and the parts shipped off to all four corners of the world, depending on the orders received. As chop-shops went, the *Workshop* was a chop-shop of the most macabre variety.

"Hush, hush," Valerie shouted.
The lecture hall became quiet.
"Before we begin," Valerie said. "I've been asked to remind you about the blood drive this afternoon. Those of you who have given blood before don't need to be told about the importance of staying hydrated, but for those of you who haven't yet had the pleasure, I'll give you some advice. Drink at least a pint of water before donating and eat a snack to maintain your blood sugar levels. The drive will take place in the refectory today. Those of you who've signed up need to be there at two sharp."
"I'll make sure I've finished eating by then," a man in the back row heckled.

"Carrying on from where we left off last time," Valerie said. "We were discussing the commercial trade in human organs. As of right now, this trade is illegal in all countries with the exception of Iran."

"Why doesn't that surprise me?" a man with a ring through his nose commented.

"Will that be all, Jeffrey?" Valerie said.

"I apologise, Dr Kyle."

"Very good. As recently as 1994 this trade was perfectly legal in India and the Philippines, but not anymore, and with the exception of Iran human organ trade remains against the law. And that leads us to our first problem. Anyone?"

A young, blond woman in the front row raised her hand.

"Lisa," Valerie urged.

"You outlaw something, and you open the door wide for criminal activity, especially when the demand is still there."

"Precisely," Valerie said. "Supply and demand. Where there's demand, someone will always step in to supply."

The door to the hall opened and two men came in and sat down right at the back. Valerie didn't comment on their timekeeping.

"From an anthropological perspective," she said. "We can trace the origins of human organ trade as far back as 600BC when the Indian surgeon Sushruta used the skin of other men and women to graft onto burns. In 348 AD Jacobus De Voragine wrote of limb transplants in his *Legenda Aurea*. Of course, the authenticity of this is up for debate, but there is little doubt that the practice of extracting body parts from one human to use for the benefit of another is extremely real."

A hand was raised in the air three rows from the back. It was one of the women who had been deep in discussion before the lecture.

"Kirsty," Valerie said. "Do you have something you wish to bring up?"

"It's happening in the city," the woman called Kirsty said.

"What exactly are you referring to?"

"Human body part trafficking. There's a place in York known as *The Workshop* and the rumour is - it's a place where corpses are brought in to be chopped up."

"Ah," Valerie said. "A good old-fashioned urban legend. We'll be discussing some more of those at length later in the term."

"It's not an urban legend," Kirsty argued. "It's real. It's actually happening right here in the city."

* * *

"Smith," DI Smyth said. "Where are we at with the recent spate of carjacking?"

Vehicle theft had risen dramatically in the city in the past few months. The cars that had been stolen were high-end models, and it was clear from the onset that this was a case of stealing to order. The people involved were organised and highly advanced.

"We're dealing with a gang that are technically adept," Smith said. "Most of the cars that were taken had top of the range security, but the thieves somehow managed to bypass this. They plan everything carefully, and so far, they've left nothing to chance. They're aware of CCTV and they're in and out in minutes. They're exceptional at what they do."

"I wasn't asking whether you're a fan of these thugs," DI Smyth said. "The Super is breathing down my neck wanting to know when we'll have a result. You are aware that his beloved Range Rover was one of the cars that was stolen."

"How could I forget?" Smith said. "It's still early days. We'll be speaking to the usual suspects and hopefully we'll get some idea of where these people are operating out of. The vehicles are taken somewhere and chopped up quickly. The turnaround is phenomenal."

His phone started to ring in his pocket, and he let it go to voicemail.

"What else do we know?" DI Smyth said.

"We don't believe the parts are being shipped abroad," DS Bridge said.

"We've had no alarm bells going off at customs."

"It's possible someone in Customs and Excise is involved," DC Moore said.

"It's not unheard of," DI Smyth said.

"No," Smith disagreed. "I don't think this gang is that stupid. To get away with exporting illegal goods you would need a whole team of bent customs officials in your pocket. The car parts are being transported within the country – probably by road."

"I think so too," DC King said. "Look at how many trucks are on the roads these days. There's no way to keep tabs on all of them."

"Going back to your usual suspects," DI Smyth said. "Who are we talking about?"

Smith nodded to the whiteboard at the back of the room.

"They're all on there."

The list wasn't a particularly long one – seven names, that was it.

"There's a name you've missed off," Bridge said.

"You're welcome to add it," Smith told him.

Bridge did.

"Are you taking the piss?" Smith said. "He's not involved in shit like that anymore."

"Once a criminal, and all that," Bridge said.

"He's kept his nose clean for years," Whitton joined in.

The name that Bridge had written was Frankie Lewis. It was true that he had been in trouble with the law once upon a time, but that was all in the past. He'd promised Smith this and Smith had believed him.

Frankie Lewis was Lucy's boyfriend's father, and he and his wife were looking after Smith's grandson for the week.

CHAPTER THREE

"Are you missing the thrill of a murder investigation, Sarge?" DC King said. She and Smith were heading south towards Fulford.

"No," Smith replied, and he meant it.

The carjacking case was mundane in comparison to a juicy murder investigation, but Smith was content to settle for it. There hadn't been a murder in the city since the *Creed* investigation and for once Smith was glad. That case had taken it out of everyone on the team and it was a relief to settle into a routine that did not involve unlawful killing.

"Have you met this Horace Nagel bloke before?" DC King said.

"We've crossed paths," Smith said. "Nagel is old school – he had old school values, and I don't think he's involved in this one."

"What's he like?"

"Like I said, I only really came across him in passing, but if you were to label him, you'd probably use the term *lovable rogue*. He wasn't into hurting people like most of the scum today – he was all about getting away with it without anyone getting injured in the process."

"He did ten years in Full Sutton for armed robbery," DC King reminded him.

"He used fake guns," Smith said. "He wouldn't have hurt anybody."

"But he didn't get away with it, did he?"

"Horace Nagel got away with it," Smith insisted. "The armed robbery botch up was just the tip of the iceberg. Look at these houses – easily a million each. He got away with a lot more than you think."

He slowed down to take in the golf estate they were driving through. The properties here were only a few years old and they were ultra-modern. Smith had been way off the mark with his estimation – most of the houses on the estate cost more than double what he'd guessed. The owners of the properties were a mixed bunch. Doctors and lawyers lived next door to football players and businessmen.

And retired criminals.

Horace Nagel looked younger than his seventy-two years. His face was tanned and the hair on his head thick. His eyes were bright blue – they were too blue, and Smith suspected that he was wearing coloured contact lenses.

"Can I help you?"

There was a hint of an accent in his voice.

Smith took out his ID. "DS Smith, and this is DC King. Can we have a word?"

"You'd better make it quick," Horace said.

He invited them in and told them to take a seat in the living room. Smith noticed that there were two suitcases against the wall in the hallway.

"Going somewhere?" he asked him.

"That's right," Horace said. "What do you want?"

"Nice place you have here. It must have set you back a bit."

"I've made a few wise business decisions in my life. Invested at the right time. Are you going to tell me why a couple of detectives are sniffing around."

"You're retired, aren't you?" Smith said.

"I'm seventy-two," Horace said. "I'd say I've earned it."

"Do you still like to keep abreast of what's going on in the city?"

"I keep my ear to the ground."

"I was wondering if you'd heard anything about a chop shop that's sprung up recently," Smith said. "A highly advanced operation."

"I've heard a few rumours. Not sure whether they're true or not."

"They're very true," Smith said. "What have you heard?"

"Nasty stuff," Horace said. "I didn't think stuff like that went on in places like York."

"Vehicles being chopped up for parts is nothing new."

"Vehicles?"

"That's right." It was DC King. "What did you think we were talking about?"

"My mistake. I thought you were referring to the rumour about the other chop shop. *The Workshop.*"

"Are you going on holiday?" Smith asked.

"Valencia," Horace said. "I've got a little place there where I like to spend the winters. I'm not as young as I used to be, and this Yorkshire cold goes right through me these days."

"You spend the winter in Spain?" DC King said.

"Have done for the past ten years. Should be pretty quiet this year what with the Brexit nonsense. Don't know what they were thinking. Luckily, I've still got my Dutch passport – the poor English bastards who have places out there have to get a visa now. Can you believe it? A visa to be able to stay in your own property. This country's gone to the dogs. If I were you, I'd get out now before it gets worse. That accent is Australian, isn't it? You've still got options, lad."

Smith wasn't interested in politics. They were getting sidetracked.

"Do you still keep in touch with the old crowd?" he said.

"Some of them," Horace replied. "Although their numbers have dwindled over the years. Look, I've got a plane to catch in a few hours – what's on your mind?"

"I was hoping you could help us with some names," Smith said. "We've got a highly advanced team of carjackers on our hands, and I'm getting heat from the people further up the food chain. One of them was a victim of this gang."

"I'm sorry to hear that," Horace said. "I sincerely hope it wasn't Jeremy Smyth, and I mean that with all the sarcasm a Dutchman can muster."

"It was, in fact."

"Good. I had a few run-ins with him back in the day. Is he still a twat?"
Smith didn't comment, although he was sorely tempted.

"These people are organised," he said. "They strike at just the right time, and they have the technical know-how to be able to bypass top of the range security measures. Can you think of anyone who fits the bill for that?"
"A few people," Horace said. "Most of them deceased. Look, I don't know why you came here, but you should have known better. I never have been, and I never will be a snitch."
"Is that some *honour amongst thieves* bullshit?" Smith said.
"Call it what you like. My driver is picking me up in twenty minutes, and I still have a bit of last-minute packing to attend to, so if there's nothing else."
"I think we're done here," Smith said. "Just a word of warning though."
"I'm listening."
"I couldn't help noticing the Land Rover in the driveway. Looks brand new."
"Straight out of the box."
"Make sure it's locked up securely," Smith said. "These people are exceptional, and that vehicle is something they might be interested in."
Horace shrugged his shoulders. "It's only a car – that's why we pay insurance, isn't it?"

He showed them out. Smith thanked him for his time and he and DC King made their way back to the car. Smith turned around halfway there.
"Just one more thing."
"You're having a laugh, aren't you?" Horace said. "Do you lot still say that?"
"What did you mean back there?" Smith said. "You mentioned something about nasty stuff – what were you talking about? You referred to a workshop."
"Just something I heard," Horace said. "Sounds more like some kind of urban legend than anything else."
"Go on."

"There's a rumour going around about this workshop. Word is, it's not your usual, run of the mill workshop. It's not cars that are being chopped up and sold off if you know what I mean."

Smith had no idea what he meant.

"Like I said," Horace said. "Probably no more than a rumour. This is the twenty-first century – we don't have human meat markets in this day and age, do we?"

CHAPTER FOUR

"I told you it was going to rain."
Gemma Hill looked skyward at the grey clouds merging overhead.
"It'll pass," her husband, John told her. "We're almost there anyway."
John and Gemma were half a mile from the caravan park in Four Lanes End. John had suggested they take a walk from the park to the air museum in Elvington. He'd always been fascinated by aviation, but when they arrived the sign outside told them the museum was closed on Mondays.

"You should have checked the museum's website before you dragged me halfway across the countryside," Gemma said.
"It was a two-mile hike," John said. "Do you want some of this tea?"
He held out the thermos. Gemma declined.

She spotted a bench up ahead.
"Let's sit down for a bit. I need to loosen the laces on my boots – I made them too tight."
"No problem," John said.

Gemma sat down but John remained standing. Something had caught his attention in the field behind the bench.
"What are you looking at?" Gemma said and set about untying the laces on her boots.
"There's something in that field," John said. "I can't make out what it is."

The first drops of rain started to fall.
"I told you it was going to rain," Jemma said.
"A few drops won't hurt you," John said. "I'm going to check out the field."
"Don't be long."

John hopped over the fence and made his way to the mysterious object in the field. He thought it could be some kind of animal. It was roughly the shape of a medium-size dog, and it was dark in colour. He approached it cautiously. It was possible that it was hurt, and John knew from experience that injured animals could be unpredictable.

As he got closer, John really didn't know what he was looking at. Whatever species of animal it was, it was nothing he'd ever come across before. The rain was falling harder now. John dared to get closer to the *thing* on the ground and then he stopped, stock-still.

His eyes studied the creature before him. Its skin was mottled in places, and there were raw lacerations running in all directions. It had no arms, legs or head, and when his eyes moved further up John felt the acid in his stomach react. A burning stream of bile shot from his mouth, and he fell to his knees. He didn't know what had happened that had led to the *thing* being here, but he did know one thing for certain – this was once a woman. The rain was now pelting down onto two small breasts.

* * *

Smith and DC King were on their way back to the station when he got the call. At first Smith couldn't make any sense of what DI Smyth was trying to tell him. He asked him to speak more clearly.
"We're not sure what we're dealing with yet," DI Smyth said. "But a man out for a walk found something in a field close to the caravan park in Four Lanes End. He thinks it's the body of a woman, but he couldn't be sure."
"Either it's a dead woman or it isn't," Smith said.
"Webber and the Forensic team are on their way. We'll know more when they've had a look, but this rain isn't going to do us any favours. Do you know the area?"
Smith told him he was familiar with it and agreed to go and check it out.

"Looks like we spoke too soon, Kerry," Smith said to DC King. "A bloke has found what he believes to be a woman's body over in Four Lanes End."
"What do we do about the carjacking gang?"

"A dead body trumps a few stolen vehicles," Smith said. "I really need a holiday."

He'd discussed it with Whitton during the *Creed* case, but she'd been dead against the idea. The girls had just started the new school term and, at the time they were in the middle of adopting Fran Rogers. It was touch and go at one stage, but in an extraordinary series of events, the decision fell in their favour and Fran was now officially a member of the Smith household.

The rain had eased off slightly when Smith turned onto Common Lane and headed for the place where the *body* had been found. Grant Webber's car was parked on the side of the narrow road and Smith parked behind it. The Head of Forensics was nowhere to be seen. A police car approached and came to a stop behind Smith's Ford Sierra. The doors opened and the PCs Griffin and Miller got out. Both of them walked over to the driver's side of Smith's car.

"Sarge," PC Miller said. "What do we know?"

"Not much right now," Smith said and got out of the car. "Reports of a dead woman. This is a pretty isolated place but there's always the danger that someone will come along. I want you and PC Griffin to stay here and make sure nobody goes anywhere near the scene."

"Where exactly is the scene?" It was PC Griffin.

"God knows," Smith said. "But Webber's car is here so it can't be far away."

"He's over there," DC King said.

She pointed to one of the fields about a hundred metres away.

"I need my eyes tested," Smith said.

The white SOC suits of Webber's team were clearly visible through the rain.

Smith opened the boot of the car and took out two suits of his own. He handed one to DC King and set about getting suited up.

"I want the road blocked off in both directions," he told the uniformed officers. "Like I said, very few people use this road, but you never know."
"It looks like the rain is getting heavier," PC Griffin said.
Smith nodded to the piggy-eyed PC. "Then you're going to get wet. Come on, Kerry."

CHAPTER FIVE

They headed for the white suits of the Forensics officers. It was hard going – the ground was boggy underfoot and Smith cursed himself for not wearing more suitable shoes. More than once, his feet sank into the sodden grass. When they got closer Smith saw that a circle of police tape had been erected around something on the ground. He couldn't make out what the tape was protecting – whatever it was had been covered with a white tarpaulin. Smith guessed that this was to shield it from the elements.

Webber spotted him and came over.
"I thought I'd seen everything."
"Go on," Smith said.
"It's definitely a female," the Head of Forensics said. "But there isn't much left of her. An ID is going to be tricky. Her arms, legs and head have been amputated."
"Jesus."
"Indeed. She has a lot of lacerations on her stomach and chest, and it looks like the injuries are fairly recent."
Smith experienced an unpleasantly warm sensation in his stomach. It was a sensation he was familiar with, and it was something that always heralded the beginning of something extremely nasty.
"Can I take a look?" he asked.
The rain stopped for a few seconds and then it started to fall again.
"I can't see why not," Webber said. "This rain has done a beautiful job of obliterating any potential evidence. We've covered her up, but I fear it was too little too late."
He looked at DC King. "Are you OK with this?"
She nodded, but she didn't seem very sure about it.
"Where's the bloke who found her?" Smith asked.

"He and his wife are staying at the Ashfield Caravan Park," Webber said. "He's in a bad way, so I asked Pete to give them a lift there. We'll get a statement from them later – they're not going anywhere."

Smith and DC King walked towards the ominous bulge underneath the tarpaulin. Smith sensed that DC King walked more slowly than she usually did, and he kept in step with her.

"You really don't have to do this," he said.

"I know," she said and increased her pace.

She walked with her head up, with purpose.

Billie Jones was taking photographs of the surrounding area. She looked up and her eyes told Smith everything he needed to know. Billie was a seasoned forensics technician – she'd seen things that would turn the stomach of most but here in this field with the rain pelting down, she looked like a woman who had recently come face to face with her worst nightmare.

Pete Richards seemed even worse. The big, bearded forensics officer's face was sickly pale, and his bloodshot eyes looked haunted. Smith wondered if he'd been crying.

"You OK?" he asked.

Pete shook his head. "Not really. I thought I'd seen the worst that humanity is capable of. Whoever did that to her needs to be exterminated."

Smith crouched down next to the tarpaulin. A pool of rainwater had gathered in one of the larger creases of the plastic. Smith splashed it away with his hand without knowing why. He sensed that DC King was behind him.

"You really don't have to see this. Billie will have taken a load of photographs."

"I want to, Sarge," she said. "I want to see it so I can get angry."

Smith thought this was a rather strange thing to say, but he kept quiet.

He reached for the edge of the tarpaulin and carefully peeled it back.

DC King let out a gasp, but she remained where she was. Smith took in what he was looking at. It wasn't nearly as bad as he'd anticipated it to be, and he wondered if this was something to be concerned about. He decided that it was because what he was observing didn't have many human aspects to it. He felt like he was looking down at a slab of meat that had slipped from a butcher's hook, and if it wasn't for the two small breasts and female hips, he wouldn't really know it was a woman.

Her skin already had the mottled bluish-black tinge that told him that rigor mortis had set it. Smith knew from experience that they would find pooling due to livor mortis on her back if they turned her over. He had no intention of doing that – what he was interested in was the lacerations on her chest and stomach. There was a long gash the entire length of her stomach and a number of smaller ones one either side of her chest. More cuts had been made in the middle of her torso.

"What do you think?" Smith asked DC King.
She didn't reply.
"Kerry," Smith said. "Are you alright?"
"She's been operated on," DC King said.
With a gloved hand she lay a finger on the woman's stomach. "I think someone has removed her vital organs."
"Let's not get ahead of ourselves," Smith said. "We can't tell that just from looking at her."
"I think that's what happened."

Later, at the post-mortem her suspicions would be confirmed. Dr Bean would discover that the common practice of removing the organs for testing purposes during the autopsy would be problematic because this woman no longer had any of her vital organs inside her. Her heart, liver, lungs and kidneys were gone.

Smith had seen enough. He assumed that DC King had too. He took hold of the tarpaulin and was about to cover the torso up again when something on the side of the body made him stop. There was a smudge of black halfway down and Smith wondered if it was a tattoo.

"That might help us identify her," he said to DC King.

She took a closer look.

"It's not a tattoo, Sarge."

"This just gets weirder and weirder," Smith said.

The smudge on the skin was in fact an almost perfect circle and when Smith's eyes focused harder he realised two things at the same time. It was an @ symbol, and it hadn't been tattooed onto her skin – the edges of the symbol were raw. The second thing that Smith registered was much more disturbing.

This woman had been branded.

CHAPTER SIX

"I think we can justify moving the carjacking gang onto the backburner for the foreseeable future," DI Smyth began the afternoon briefing.
The nods from the detectives inside the small conference room told him they agreed.
"Smith," DI Smyth said. "I believe it wasn't pretty."
"I'm still trying to process what she was subjected to, boss," Smith said.
"Her head, arms and legs were amputated, and I can't figure out why someone would do that. Kerry and me believe her internal organs were also removed. She had numerous incisions that looked like surgery wounds. She also had what looked like branding on her right side."
"Branding?" DC Moore said.
"An @ symbol," Smith elaborated. "God knows what it means, but I reckon that's why she was left to be found. Whoever did that to her wanted us to see what had been done to her."
"Let's not be hasty here," DI Smyth said.
"Think about it," Smith said. "You chop off someone's head, arms and legs and remove their vital organs there isn't really much left of them to dispose of, is there? Why bother to go to the effort of dumping the remains of the body when all you'd really need is a household refuse bag?"
"Do you think they wanted us to see the branding?" Bridge wondered.
"Why bother doing that to her if you don't want it noticed?" Smith said.
"I feel ill," DC Moore said. "Do you think we've got a monster on the loose?"
Nobody offered any comment on this.

"As of yet," DI Smyth said. "We don't have an ID and obtaining one is going to be extremely difficult. We have no fingerprints to look at, no dental records and the only feasible way we're going to be able to identify her is through DNA analysis."

"And only if someone reports her missing and we've got something to compare that DNA with," Bridge pointed out.

"Exactly," DI Smyth said. "And that's going to make life extremely difficult for us. We cannot even begin to hypothesise about a motive when we have no idea who the victim is. I've got uniforms sifting through missing persons, so hopefully that will give us something. Dr Bean has also promised to fast-track the post-mortem."

"Kenny will be able to give us an idea about her age," Smith said. "I don't think she was very old."

"Moving on," DI Smyth said. "The man who found the body wasn't able to give us much. John and Gemma Hill were staying in a caravan at the Ashfield Park, and they'd just come from the aviation museum when John spotted something suspicious. He went to take a look and that's when he made the grisly discovery."

"Are there many other people staying at the caravan park?" Smith asked. "It's not exactly the holiday season."

"We'll be checking it out," DI Smyth said. "That park is the closest thing to human habitation where the woman's remains were found. Someone might have seen something. There is only one road running past the fields."

"Common Lane," Smith remembered. "You can either access it from Hull Road in the north or Elvington Lane to the south. It's not much more than a gravel track and there's usually not much traffic on it."

"Are we assuming she was brought there by car?" DC Moore said.

"It's the logical assumption to make, Harry," DI Smyth said. "Whoever dumped the body will have had to walk the last bit of the way, but I say they parked up where our officers parked earlier and took her to the field where she was found."

"Unfortunately," Smith said. "The downpour earlier will have washed away any potential evidence. It's the first rain we've had for over a week and any shoeprints or tyre tracks will have been washed away."

"Perhaps the killer kept an eye on the weather forecast," DC Moore suggested.

"Hardly likely," Smith said. "The weather forecast in Yorkshire is about as reliable as Uncle Jeremy's intellect."

"That's enough," DI Smyth said. "And how many times do I have to remind you that it's Superintendent Smyth to you?"

"I'm stumped," Bridge said. "Does anyone have any theories about why she was mutilated like that?"

"There is a damn good reason for it," Smith said. "Chopping off someone's head, arms and legs is not only messy – it's time consuming, and it would need to take place somewhere secluded. You don't do that in a residential area."

"You'd probably need specialised tools," Whitton said. "Bone saws and other surgical equipment."

DI Smyth's phone started to ring. He looked at the screen and sighed. "I'd better take this. It's the Super. He's been hounding me day and night about the progress in the carjacking investigation. I'll be back in a minute." He got up and left the room.

"Someone went to a hell of a lot of trouble here," Smith said.

"The branding is bugging me," DC King said. "Why brand her with the @ symbol?"

"It's the *at* sign," DC Moore said. "Nothing more."

"The branding has to mean something," Smith said. "Otherwise, why bother?"

"Where do you think the rest of her ended up?" Whitton put forward.

"Webber didn't find any body parts anywhere near where she was found," Smith said.

"They could have been dumped in various parts of the city," DC Moore said. "It's happened before where a body is chopped up and left in different places to throw the police off the scent."

Smith stared at him.

DC Moore held up his arms. "It's been documented. It makes our job much harder."

"That's not what I'm thinking about, Harry," Smith said. "We're not going to find them."

"We don't know that," Bridge said.

"No," Smith said. "We're not going to find them because whoever did this to her has kept them."

CHAPTER SEVEN

"The Super isn't a happy man," DI Smyth told Smith in the canteen.
Smith took a drink of coffee. "Tell someone who cares."
"He wants his car found," DI Smyth said. "And he doesn't think we're doing enough about it."
"His precious Range Rover is no longer in one piece. It was chopped up as soon as it arrived at the chop-shop."
"He's suggested that we split into two separate teams," DI Smyth said. "One task force to tackle the recent murder and the other to focus on the carjacking gang."
"Fuck that," Smith said. "The car thieves can wait. We've got a nasty bastard out there who likes to chop up more important things than cars, and we need everyone we have working on that. Tell Uncle Jeremy we're working round the clock on the carjackers. He won't even twig that we're not."
"You're right, of course," DI Smyth said. "Where do you suggest we go from here?"
"I don't know, boss. Horace Nagel mentioned something when we spoke to him earlier."
"Horace Nagel?"
"Gentleman thief. He was a legend in his day. He's retired now, but when me and Kerry went to talk to him about possible names for the people involved in the chop shop, he got the wrong end of the stick at first. He thought we were referring to a completely different kind of chop shop. He said he'd heard a rumour about some kind of meat market."
"Is he reliable?" DI Smyth said. "It's possible he was winding you up."
"People have tried to wind me up plenty of times," Smith said. "I didn't get the impression Nagel was taking the piss."
"What exactly did he say to you about this meat market?"

"He talked about an urban legend that was doing the rounds," Smith said. "And he mentioned something called *The Workshop*. It's like a vehicle chop shop but it's not cars being stripped for their parts. I think it might be worth looking into."

"OK," DI Smyth said. "Speak to this Nagel character again."

"That might be a bit of a problem," Smith said. "We caught him as he was on his way to the airport. He's got a place in Spain, and he'll be spending the winter there."

"It's alright for some."

"Crime pays, boss. Crime definitely pays."

* * *

"What does it feel like?" Noel Moore asked. "Does it hurt?"

"You hardly feel it," Kirsty Davies told him.

The third-year students were on their way to the refectory to give blood. A group of university students had started the initiative a few years ago and the drives had grown from strength to strength. The last blood drive held at York University had attracted four dozen young men and women and the numbers were growing.

"I've given blood since I was sixteen," Kirsty said.

"God," Noel said. "Most people that age are busy getting high and going on dates. You're weird."

"I was contacted personally," Kirsty said. "Because of my blood type. I have AB negative and fewer than one percent of the population have that type."

"I would have thought there wouldn't be much demand for it then."

"No," Kirsty said. "There isn't much AB negative blood in the banks, so if someone with that blood type needs a transfusion, it's difficult to locate some."

"Are you sure it doesn't hurt?" Noel said.

"You'll feel a slight pin prick," Kirsty said. "And as long as you're not squeamish and scared of the sight of blood, all you'll experience is a bit of fatigue afterwards. Don't worry – they'll look after you."

Noel flipped the cap off his bottle of water and took a long sip.
"What did you mean earlier at the lecture when you spoke about that urban legend?"

"*The Workshop*?" Kirsty said.

"What is it?"

"They say it's some place where bodies are taken to be chopped up."

"And you believe it?"

"You heard what Dr Kyle said about human organ trafficking. It's real."

"But this is York?" Noel said.

"So? This kind of thing can happen anywhere."

"I don't believe it," Noel said. "I think it's a load of bullshit dreamt up by some bored kids."

Kirsty laughed. "I think so too."

"What? But you said…"

"I wanted to see what kind of reaction I got. Are you ready?"

A little over an hour later Noel Moore was feeling a bit sick. The unit of blood that had been extracted from his vein had left him exhausted and nauseous. He'd been advised to get some rest and he'd been assured that the nausea would pass.

Kirsty Davies said goodbye and exited the university campus. The students who'd given blood were exempt from classes for the rest of the day, and Kirsty planned to go straight to the house she shared with three other students. She headed east on Kimberley Drive and walked past the sports village. The rain from earlier was a distant memory and the sky now had patches of blue in it.

Kirsty stopped at the row of shops and went inside the bakery. She was always peckish after giving blood. She bought a Cornish pasty and took the first bite before she'd even left the shop. She carried on in the direction of Hull Road and ate as she walked. She'd just passed Diamond Wood when she heard the sound of a vehicle approaching behind her. The van drove past and stopped up ahead. Kirsty dumped the pasty packet in the rubbish bin next to where it had stopped.

"It's Miss one in a hundred and sixty-seven."
This caught Kirsty's attention. Those odds were imprinted on her brain – they were the odds of someone having type AB negative blood. She vaguely recognised the man. He'd also given blood at the university, but he hadn't been there today.

"I bet nobody has ever called you that before."
Kirsty thought he had a friendly face. He was tall and thin, and he was dressed in jeans and a T-Shirt with a photograph of a warthog on it.
He held out his hand. "Luke."
He smiled, and Kirsty noticed his dimples.
She shook the hand. "Kirsty."
"I know," Luke said. "I've been stalking you. Well, not really – I saw you at the blood drive last term and I was hoping to see you again."
"You weren't there today."
"I had to help my Gran move to her new lodgings."
Kirsty thought this was a strange way to describe it, but she liked the way he talked. Luke was very different to any of the other students she'd met.

"Can I give you a lift?" he asked. "I've got the van for another hour – I've paid for it, so I might as well abuse it."
"I live half a mile from here," Kirsty told him.
"I'm sure she'll make it," Luke said and patted the side of the white van. "She's not that old."

"I didn't mean…"

"I'm messing with you," Luke said. "Come on and hop in. I don't bite. You can tell me about your special blood on the way."

Kirsty laughed. "OK then."

Luke walked around the van and opened the passenger door for her. "Make yourself comfortable, Miss one in a hundred and sixty-seven."

He handed her a bottle of water and she was grateful for it. The Cornish pasty had dried out her mouth and she opened the bottle and took a long drink.

Kirsty Davies was blissfully unaware then that her rare blood type was about to throw her headlong into the stuff of nightmares.

CHAPTER EIGHT

"We've got the preliminary post-mortem results in," DI Smyth said.
It was getting late, but he'd decided to have a final briefing for the day.
"The woman found earlier today is someone between the ages of twenty and thirty. Unfortunately, Dr Bean couldn't be any more accurate than that. He's based his conclusions on the condition of the woman's epidermal layers and nothing more. He wasn't able to examine the internal organs because there weren't any to examine."
DC Moore let out a gasp and apologised straight away.

"It's fine, Harry," DI Smyth said. "We are allowed to react to this – we're only human. The heart, liver, lungs and both kidneys were removed. According to the report, the incisions made in order to carry out the transplants were rather crude in nature. This wasn't carried out by someone with experience in surgical procedures. Apart from the fact that they knew where the organs were located, there's nothing to suggest we're looking for someone with medical expertise beyond that which you could find on the Internet."

"Do we know if she was alive when the organs were removed?" Smith asked.
"That's going to take time to determine," DI Smyth said. "All we have right now is the prelim report."
"I don't think she was," DC Moore said. "Surely removing them would kill her."
"Eventually," Smith agreed. "But if the organs were removed to sell on, they will have had to be in good condition."
"Whoa," DC Moore said. "What are you saying – she was killed for her organs?"
"It's worth considering. I'm just wondering if this has something to do with

The Workshop the grapevine of the city is talking about."

"*Workshop?*" Whitton said.

"It's something Horace Nagel mentioned. Even though he's retired, he still keeps his eyes and ears open, and he spoke about a chop-shop that doesn't involve stolen cars."

"That's ridiculous." It was Bridge. "Stuff like that does not happen in Yorkshire."

"How many times have we said that over the years?" Smith said. "*Stuff like that doesn't happen in Yorkshire?* Stuff like that does happen here – I've lost count of how many times we've been there and got the fucking T-Shirt."

"I still think you're barking up the wrong tree, Sarge," DC Moore said.

"Do you have any better theories? Perhaps there's a cannibal roaming the city who likes to gorge on human organs. Or maybe we're dealing with an escaped lunatic who is so full of pent-up rage, he feels the need to dismember women and keep their body parts as trophies."

"It's getting late," DI Smyth said. "Dr Bean did a perfunctory examination of the amputation sites. Thankfully, he didn't go into too much detail – I for one could do without that right now, but he could determine that all of the amputations were carried out using a surgical saw or something similar."

"Perhaps that's something to look into," Bridge said.

"It's not," Smith argued. "I could be wrong, but I bet you can get your hands on a surgical saw from the Internet."

"You're not wrong, Sarge," DC Moore said. "You can buy them on eBay and we all know what a dead end that is."

"Does anyone have anything to add before we conclude for the day?" DI Smyth said.

"Don't have nightmares," Smith said.

"Very funny, Sarge," DC Moore said.

He was the first out the door.

"I need a drink," Bridge said.

"No hot date tonight?" Smith said.

"I'm taking a break from relationships for a while."

"I've seen everything now."

"Do you fancy a pint?" Bridge asked.

He picked up his phone and stood up.

"Not tonight," Smith said. "I need to get my head round what happened today, and I need to do that sober."

"I'll see you at home," Whitton said.

Smith nodded. Whitton and Bridge left the room together. DI Smyth followed them out.

"Is everything alright?" Smith asked DC King.

She'd made no effort to get up.

"Kerry?" Smith said. "You didn't say a word at the briefing. Are you OK?"

She shook her head. "No, I don't think I am. It didn't bother me at the time – it really didn't, but now I can't stop seeing it. I can't stop seeing her."

"It wasn't something we were expecting to have to deal with."

"I thought I was doing the right thing," DC King said. "You said I didn't have to look at her, but I did anyway. I thought if I saw her, it would drive me to catch the people responsible. I thought it would make me angry and that would help."

"Don't you feel angry?" Smith said. "I'm pretty fucking fuming myself."

If Smith hoped to lighten the mood, he'd failed miserably.

DC King looked at him with red-rimmed eyes. Smith wondered if she was going to cry.

"I don't even feel angry," she said. "I feel nothing – numb, is how I feel."

"It'll pass," Smith said. "Trust me when I say it'll pass. Go home and get some sleep. If you feel like talking about it, you know where I am."

DC King stood up now. She nodded to Smith and left him alone in the small conference room. Smith watched her go. The image of the naked female torso came back to him, and he didn't blame DC King for reacting the way she had. Nobody should have to deal with something like that. The dismembered body of a young woman wasn't something they told you about in training. Smith suddenly changed his mind about that beer. It was exactly what he felt like right now.

CHAPTER NINE

He caught up to Bridge in the car park.

"Are you still up for that pint?"

"What's brought about the change of heart?" Bridge said.

"A bloke is allowed to change his mind these days," Smith said. "This is 2021 – it's the age of equality."

"Where did you have in mind?"

"Guess."

"Hog's Head it is then. I'll see you there."

There was no indication that the heavens had opened earlier as Smith drove. The tarmac on the roads was bone-dry and he wondered if the rain had been sent to test them. It couldn't have happened at a worse time. Everything they could hope to get from the woman's torso had been washed clean, leaving only what was obvious to the naked eye.

Smith was halfway to the Hog's Head when something occurred to him. Dr Bean hadn't mentioned anything about the branding on the woman's side. He turned into a side road, parked the car and dialled the Head of Pathology's mobile number.

Dr Bean picked up straight away. "Why am I surprised to hear from you?"

"How are you, Kenny?" Smith said.

"Halfway out the door. What can I do for you?"

"We discussed your prelim post-mortem report," Smith told him. "There was nothing about the branding – the *at* symbol."

"It's actually the *at sign*," Dr Bean said. "It's a common mistake."

"Kenny," Smith said. "What did you make of it?"

"What part of *prelim* report do you not understand?"

"I get that," Smith said. "But you must have some idea about that branding."

"It was done rather crudely. Don't quote me on this but I'd say it was burned onto her skin with something similar to the branding irons used to denote ownership of livestock."

"Interesting."

"Of course it is," Dr Bean said. "Is there anything else you need from me before I walk out of the hospital and switch my phone off for the night?"

"I don't think so," Smith said. "Thanks Kenny."

The next call was to his wife. Whitton didn't feel like an evening at the Hog's Head. There was a documentary she was keen to watch, and she wanted nothing more than to curl up in front of the television. Smith told her he probably wouldn't be late, but he couldn't promise anything.

* * *

Bridge was already there when Smith got to the Hog's Head and Smith could see he'd been busy in his absence. He was talking to a couple of women at the bar. Smith watched as the shorter of the two took out her phone and she and Bridge proceeded to exchange numbers. Smith smiled – Bridge never ceased to amaze him. He walked to the opposite side of the bar and caught the attention of the barman. He was new.

"Pint of Theakston please."

"Coming up. Are you going to have something to eat?"

"Probably," Smith said.

"I'll get you a menu."

"No need," Smith told him. "I've been coming here for over a decade, and I always have the same thing. If you could sort me out with that Theakston, that would be great."

"Coming up," the barman said once more.

"I didn't see you there," Bridge said.

He'd walked over without Smith realising.

"I could see you were in the middle of something," Smith said. "So much for the relationship hiatus."

"A bloke has to keep his options open," Bridge said.

The barman placed Smith's beer on the counter. Smith took it and finished half of it in one go. Then he drained the rest of it for good measure. The barman nodded. "Impressive. Can I get you another one?"

Smith replied in the affirmative.

"Is Marge around?"

"She's having a lie down," the barman said. "She's not feeling too great."

"Nothing serious I hope?"

"I think it's one of those change of season flu things. I'll bring your pint over."

"Kenny reckons the branding on the dead woman is something similar to the branding you see on cattle and pigs," Smith said at the table.

"Can we talk about something else?" Bridge asked. "I really don't feel like discussing this tonight."

"Just hear me out. He's branding them for a damn good reason."

"Two things," Bridge said. "We don't know we're dealing with a man and there's only been one victim. *Them* is plural."

"I reckon there'll be more. I don't know why – I just know."

"Can we please talk about something else?" Bridge said.

"Who's *your* latest victim?" Smith humoured him. "Who was the short blond at the bar?"

"Olivia," Bridge said and grinned. "Don't you think that's the most beautiful name you've ever heard?"

"You say that about all of them," Smith said.

"It's like something out of Shakespeare."

"Are you going to eat something?" Smith asked.

"That scampi special looks good."

"I'm going to have a steak and ale pie."

"That makes a change."

"I know what I like," Smith said.

He put the order in at the bar and returned to the table.

"Kerry's in a bit of a bad way," he said.

"Was it that bad?"

"I expected it to be worse," Smith admitted. "It's hard to explain, but I think it's because she no longer looked human. More like a slab of meat."

"I'm starting to worry about you. I would have thought that would make it worse."

Smith shrugged his shoulders. "It is what it is, but Kerry is taking it badly."

"Perhaps she should speak to someone."

"I offered to be there for her if she needed to talk."

"No offence," Bridge said. "But what I meant was she should speak to a professional."

"A shrink?"

"Something like that."

The food arrived and Smith decided it was better not to think about the dead woman. The steak and ale pie looked different somehow – it was smaller than usual, and when Smith cut into it, he realised there was hardly any gravy. It even tasted different, and he wondered if Marge was losing her touch. He left half of it uneaten.

"Was something wrong with the pie?" the waiter asked when he came to clear the table.

"It didn't taste like it usually does," Smith said.

"It's a new recipe."

"I'm surprised Marge changed her recipe. I've been eating her pies for years."

"It was Pete's idea."

"The manager?" Smith remembered.

"That's right. He thought the place needed to make some changes. He makes the steak and ale pies himself now. They're proving to be very popular."

"Well you can tell Pete," Smith said. "I won't be ordering another one unless it's made by Marge."

"I'll make sure he's made aware of it. Can I get you anything else?"

Smith ordered another Theakston for himself and another pint of lager for Bridge.

"Can you believe it?" he said. "Those pies are the main reason I come here. I'm surprised Marge agreed to let the manager change the recipe."

"Why don't you ask him about it," Bridge said and nodded to the man walking over to their table.

Smith had only met Pete a few times before but each time he'd always got a bad vibe off him. He didn't like him at all.

"I believe you have a problem with the steak and ale pie," Pete said.

"Where do you want me to begin?" Smith said. "The pastry was as dry as a wombat's arse crack – the steak was tougher than an emu's toenail and I couldn't taste any of the ale. The gravy was non-existent."

"I was under the impression that you were a police detective."

"What's your point?" Smith said.

"I didn't know you were a secret food critic."

"There's nothing secret about it, mate," Smith said. "I know what I like, and that sorry excuse for a pie isn't it. Why change a recipe that's proven to be a winner for over a decade?"

"Because sometimes, change is necessary. The Hog's Head has been stuck in a rut for years, and I intend to do something about that."

"By fucking up a pie that people loved?" Smith couldn't believe what he was hearing.

"I'll have you know," Pete said. "The new recipe is proving to be very popular – especially with our younger patrons. I've reduced the ale quantity so there's not so much alcohol in the pie."

"I'll speak to Marge about it."

"Good luck," Pete said. "She's more than happy to take a back seat and let me get on with things. Will there be anything else?"

Smith didn't think it was worth wasting any more time arguing with a man who couldn't be reasoned with. He asked for the bill.

"What a dickhead. I can't believe he's messed with something as sacred as Marge's steak and ale pies."

"Don't get so worked up about it," Bridge said. "It's only a pie."

"That's like saying the Minster is only an old church," Smith said. "Marge's pies are part of the charm of this city."

"You're getting old."

"This has seriously pissed me off. I got a good mind not to pay for the fucking pie."

Bridge's phone beeped to tell him he'd received a message. He swiped the screen and smiled.

"That's my cue to call it a night."

"Olivia?" Smith guessed.

"You got it in one."

Bridge took out his wallet and put thirty pounds on the table.

"That's too much," Smith told him.

"It'll cover the pie you're so cut up about," Bridge said. "I'll see you in the morning."

CHAPTER TEN

Smith unlocked the door and went inside his house. He could hear the sound of the television in the living room – Whitton was still up.
He went in and sat down next to her. "You'll never guess what?"
"I'm sure you're going to tell me."
"That prick of a manager has only gone and changed the recipe for the steak and ale pie at the Hog's Head."
"Oh my God," Whitton said with exaggerated drama. "Call the police – he needs to be arrested for defacing a piece of local heritage."
"It's not funny, Erica. When I complained about it he wouldn't even listen to reason."
"It's only a pie."
"It's..." Smith began. "I give up. I'm going outside for a smoke."

The sky outside was clear, without a cloud in the sky and the temperature had plummeted. Smith wondered if this was the first of the autumn cold snaps. It had to happen sooner or later. He lit a cigarette, and his thoughts drifted from the terrible pie to the mutilated corpse of the woman. Smith couldn't imagine how one human being could do that to another human being. It was worse than anything he'd seen before, and he thought he'd seen everything.

The back door opened, and the dogs shuffled outside. Theakston sniffed the cold air and made his way to the bottom of the garden. He did what he needed to do in no time and went back inside the house. The aged Bull Terrier wasn't a big fan of the cold. Fred lingered longer. The gruesome Pug wasn't fazed by the low temperatures.

"What do you think, Fred?" Smith said. "Do you reckon there's any truth in this *Workshop* urban legend?"

Fred didn't offer an opinion. He collapsed at Smith's feet and proceeded to drool all over his shoes.

"I'll take that as a yes then," Smith said.

He decided that it was worth digging a bit deeper.

Then an idea began to form inside his head. It was a plan that would enable him to kill two birds with one stone, and Smith was particularly fond of those kind of plans. He finished his cigarette and went back inside the house to get Whitton's opinion on it.

She was in the kitchen. "Do you want some coffee?"

"I'd love some," Smith said. "I've come up with an idea."

"Why do I get the feeling that I'm not going to like this?"

"Hear me out," Smith said. "How do you feel about popping over to Spain for a few days?"

"I think it's the worst idea you've ever had," Whitton said. "In case you've forgotten, we're in the middle of a murder investigation."

"Of course I haven't forgotten. The trip will be related to the investigation. Horace Nagel knows something about this *Workshop* and he just happens to be in Valencia for the winter. Think about it – we can get away for a bit and do a bit of investigative work while we're at it."

"The DI will never authorise it," Whitton pointed out. "There is no way he'll agree to using resources for a trip to Spain to speak to a known criminal."

"Then I'll pay for it myself. We need a holiday, and I'm convinced that Nagel knows a hell of a lot more than he let on to me and Kerry."

Whitton spooned some coffee into two mugs and added hot water. "What about the girls? We can't just swan off and leave them alone."

"Lucy and Darren can help out," Smith said. "I'll leave Darren my car, and it's not like he's got much else on now he's left college. Your mum and dad will be happy to help out too. And with Andrew at Darren's parents' house for the week, it'll make life easier for them."

"It's a really bad idea."

"Sleep on it," Smith said. "This is exactly what we need right now."

* * *

Kirsty Davies woke with a throbbing headache. She was feeling disorientated, and her mouth was incredibly dry. She opened her eyes, but darkness remained. She had no idea where she was. A few snippets of memory came back to her. She remembered the blood drive and she remembered leaving the university campus and heading home.

Had she bought a Cornish pasty on the way? She thought so, but she couldn't be absolutely sure. Her recollection of what happened after that was hazy. There had been a van and a peculiar young man. She recalled accepting a lift but everything after that was a blur.

Someone coughed close by, but Kirsty couldn't see who it was. Her eyes hadn't yet adjusted to the blackness inside the room she was in. She was aware of movement behind her, and she felt cold hands on her face.
"What are you doing?"
Whoever was in there with her remained quiet. Kirsty sensed a slight pressure on her eyes – the pressure increased and then she felt something at the back of her head. Someone had blindfolded her.

Even though she couldn't see, she was aware of a change in the lighting. The blindfold was thick but still she could sense that a light had been switched on inside the room she was in. Kirsty tried to move her arms and that's when she realised that they were strapped to something. There was something irritating her right wrist and if she had the luxury of sight, she would see that it was an IV drip. It was feeding a saline solution into her veins.

"What do you want?" Kirsty said.

"You are in possession of a rather valuable commodity."

There was a hint of an accent in the voice, but Kirsty couldn't place it. It could be French or possibly German.

"Why are you doing this?"

"It is nothing personal."

Kirsty decided that her captor was definitely German.

"You will be well looked after, and you will feel no pain. Is there anything you require to make you more comfortable?"

"Just let me go," Kirsty said. "What do you want from me?"

She sensed that the person in the room with her had moved closer. She felt a tickle as a hand touched her wrist and she was aware of a quiet *pop* as the tube in the cannula was removed and replaced with something else.

"Where am I?" Kirsty asked again.

She gasped as what felt like liquid ice crept up her arms. The frozen flow reached her chest, and she could feel herself drifting off.

"You're in *The Workshop*."

The voice sounded far away.

"For now, you'll sleep."

Kirsty couldn't hear the voice anymore. The fast-acting Propofol had done exactly what it was designed to do, and she was already deep in a dreamless sleep.

CHAPTER ELEVEN

Smith opened his eyes, and something immediately occurred to him – he hadn't dreamt. He couldn't remember the last time that had happened, and he wondered if there was a reason for it. He didn't have the chance to dwell on it. An ungodly scream from downstairs caused him to jump out of bed, and he went to see what was going on.

"You bad dog."

Whitton was glaring at Theakston. The Bull Terrier was cowering next to the table in the kitchen with his ears back. He spotted Smith and crept up to him.

"What did he do?" Smith asked Whitton.

She nodded to the table. The remains of what looked like scrambled egg was spread all over the corner of it. There was an overturned plate on the floor with more egg around it.

"I put the plate down and went to make some coffee," Whitton said. "The little shit was up on the table in a flash."

Smith started to laugh. "There's still life in the old boy yet."

"It's not funny, Jason. Look at the mess he's made. He needs to learn some manners. You need to train him."

"He's a Bull Terrier," Smith reminded her.

"He's a bad dog," Whitton crouched down next to the cowering brute. "You're a bad dog."

"No harm done. Are the girls up yet?"

"I haven't heard them."

"I'll go and make some noise upstairs," Smith said. "I didn't get the chance to use the bathroom with all the commotion going on down here."

"I'm serious, Jason," Whitton said. "That dog needs to learn some manners."

"I'll have a word with him. My bladder is about to burst."

Five minutes later he sat at the kitchen table with a cup of coffee. He'd scraped up the mess of scrambled eggs and Theakston was now being punished by being locked outside in the back garden. Laura and Fran came in at the same time. Laura had her school sweater on inside out again and the girls were giggling.

"What's so funny?" Smith asked them.

Fran nudged Laura and whispered something in her ear.

"Your jumper's on inside out," Smith told Laura.

She didn't reply.

Whitton came in and told her the same thing. Still, Laura remained silent. She walked over to Smith with her eyes focused on nothing in particular. Fran giggled again.

"What's got into you?" Smith asked Laura.

She fixed him with unblinking eyes.

"I see dead people."

"Laura," Whitton said. "That's enough."

"I see dead people," Laura said once more.

Smith nodded. "Welcome to my world, kid."

"Jason." Whitton's voice was much louder now.

He shrugged his shoulders. "I reckon we should have a word with Darren about what sort of movies he lets them watch. Speaking of which – I thought he'd be ready to take them to school. It's not like he's got anything else to do."

Right on cue, the front door opened, and Lucy and Darren came into the kitchen.

"Your sweater is on inside out again," Lucy told Laura.

"Are you ready?" Darren asked.

"Girls," Whitton said. "Wait outside – we want to talk to Darren and Lucy."

"It's cold out there," Laura protested.

"It won't take long," Whitton said.

"What have you been letting the girls watch at your place?" Smith said when Laura and Fran were out of earshot.

"Nothing too grisly," Darren said.

"So, Laura telling me that she sees dead people has nothing to do with something you've let them watch on TV?"

"Oh that." It was Lucy.

"Oh that," Whitton repeated. "Jason might think it's funny, but I don't."

"It was just *The Sixth Sense*," Darren explained. "It's not that scary."

"The girls are too young to watch stuff like that."

"It won't happen again," Lucy promised.

"Make sure it doesn't," Smith said. "You're going to be late."

"Can I borrow your car?" Darren said.

"You can walk," Whitton replied. "Get out of here."

"You take things far too seriously," Smith said.

"One of us has to," Whitton said. "Girls their age shouldn't be watching horror films."

"*The Sixth Sense* isn't a proper horror film," Smith argued. "It's more of a psychological, mental mind-fuck thing."

"That makes it so much better."

"You must admit that Laura was very convincing."

"They're little girls, Jason," Whitton said. "They've been through so much and horror films are not suitable viewing for them. There's enough horror in this world without actively seeking it out."

"I'm going to bring up the trip to Spain with the boss," Smith said.

"I thought we'd discussed that," Whitton said.

"I don't recall doing that. I asked you to think about it, and as far as I can see there isn't much to consider. A bloke who can probably shed some light on this *Workshop* happens to be in Spain, and we need a break away from the city. We can have a working holiday. Do you remember when we went to Tenerife?"

"I haven't thought about that for a very long time."

"I remember it well."

"So do I," Whitton said. "I remember you frozen in time on the beach while I was busy almost drowning."

"That wasn't my fault. Come on – a few days in Valencia will be just what the doctor ordered."

"You're not going to give up, are you?"

"Nope," Smith said. "What do you think?"

"OK," Whitton said. "If you can manage to persuade the DI, I'm in."

CHAPTER TWELVE

"Absolutely not."

DI Smyth didn't even stop to think about it.

"I will not allocate funds for a wild goose chase," he added.

"Think about it, boss," Smith said. "What have we got at the moment – sweet FA. We have no idea what this *Workshop* is and we don't have a clue where it is. Horace Nagel can help us."

"It's still early days," DI Smyth said. "We've barely started with the investigation."

"He can help us. He knows more about it than he told us yesterday. Let me and Whitton go and talk to him."

"There are such things as telephones," DI Smyth said. "The man is in Spain – he's not having a sabbatical in Timbuktu."

"I don't think he'll talk to me on the phone. That's why we need to catch him unawares. It's two days, three max."

"I can't justify the expense."

"Then I'd like to put in a request for some leave," Smith said. "Whitton will do the same. We've both got plenty of holiday owed to us."

DI Smyth ran his hands through his hair.

"I'm losing hair by the handful because of you, do you realise that?"

"Your hair looks fine to me, boss," Smith said. "How about it? Me and Whitton go and speak to Nagel, and it won't cost York CID a cent."

"Two days," DI Smyth said. "You've got two days, and no more than two days."

"I knew you'd come to your senses in the end," Smith said. "There's a flight from Leeds Bradford to Valencia this afternoon at two. I've provisionally booked it."

"How did you know I was going to agree to this hairbrained plan of yours?"

"Sixth sense, boss," Smith said. "That's why they pay me the big bucks."
"I want a progress update twice a day," DI Smyth said. "And if you do manage to get anything relevant from this Nagel character, I want to be the first to know about it."
"That goes without saying."
"And you will be back here in York on Thursday," DI Smyth said. "Is that clear?"
"As clear as Uncle Jeremy's garage now his precious Range Rover is no longer parked in it."
"That's not funny, Smith," DI Smyth said.
He didn't even try to hide the grin on his face.
"If you say so, boss," Smith said. "I'd better get started with packing and stuff."
"Bring back something useful."
"I'll try my best," Smith said. "One more thing."
"You're pushing your luck now."
"Kerry isn't handling the case too well. The body yesterday spooked her a bit, and I think it might be an idea for her to talk to someone."
"I'll have a word with her. Keep me up to date."

* * *

DI Smyth explained the reason for Smith and Whitton's absence in the morning briefing.
"It's alright for some," Bridge said. "I wouldn't mind a holiday in Spain right now."
"It is not a holiday," DI Smyth said. "They'll be working, and they will be back on Thursday. In the meantime, I've recruited some extra bodies. Baldwin and PC Griffin will be temporarily assigned to the team while Smith and Whitton are away."

"Is that such a good idea, sir?" DC Moore said. "Baldwin's alright but that Griffin bloke is a bit of a know-it-all."

"Be that as it may," DI Smyth said. "He's proven himself and he's keen to learn. It's not up for debate. They'll be joining us later this morning."

The door to the room opened and PC Griffin came in.

"Sorry to interrupt."

"I thought you were tied up with something," DI Smyth said.

"I was, sir," PC Griffin said. "I was busy taking a look through recent missing persons and another one came in five minutes ago."

"Go on."

"Kirsty Davies. Twenty-two. She's a third-year student at the university and one of her housemates reported her missing because she didn't come home yesterday."

"Students are unpredictable," DC Moore said.

"Apparently, Kirsty isn't," PC Griffin said. "The housemate said she would have called to let her know she wasn't going to be coming home. She's extremely concerned."

"When did this housemate last see Kirsty?" DC King said.

"Yesterday morning. They walked to the campus together."

"The timing doesn't fit," Bridge said. "If she was seen yesterday morning, she can't be the woman found over by Four Lanes End."

"She could be a potential victim," DC King said.

"She's a young woman who didn't come home after class," Bridge said. "There could be a million reasons for that. It doesn't make her a missing person."

"In light of recent developments," DI Smyth said. "We have no option but to take it seriously. Is the housemate still here?"

"Yes, sir," PC Griffin said. "I asked her to wait so someone could talk to her."

"Good call," DI Smyth said. "You did the right thing."

"Bridge," DI Smyth. "Do you want to do the honours?"

"Me?" Bridge said. "Can one of the uniforms get a statement from her? We've got more important matters to discuss."

"It won't take long."

"She seems genuine, Sarge," PC Griffin said. "I'm quite perceptive where things like that are concerned."

Bridge glared at him but stood up anyway. "This had better not be a waste of time."

CHAPTER THIRTEEN

The woman waiting in the interview room looked extremely ill at ease. She'd given her name as Jean Bradley, and she observed Bridge as though he was about to physically assault her.

He sat down opposite her. "My name is DS Bridge. Are you alright?"

Jean nodded.

"Have you been offered anything to drink?"

"The odd bloke in uniform already asked me."

Bridge deduced that she was referring to PC Griffin.

"This is the first time I've ever been in a police station," Jean said.

"It's nothing like what you see on TV, is it?" Bridge said. "Relax, you have nothing to worry about. You came to report your housemate missing, is that correct?"

"It's not like Kirsty," Jean said. "It's not like her to stay out without telling me."

"When did you last see her?"

"Yesterday morning. We walked to the campus together."

"What are you studying?" Bridge asked.

"Political Science."

"Is Kirsty doing the same degree?"

"No," Jean said. "She's in her third year of a Psychology degree."

"Are you sure she didn't mention anything about staying overnight somewhere?" Bridge said.

"Definitely not. I would have remembered."

"Does she have a boyfriend?"

"No," Jean said. "She's totally dedicated to her studies. She's at the top of all her classes."

"Is it possible she could have met up with someone?" Bridge said. "A friend, perhaps and she ended up staying the night there?"

"She would have called to let me know."

Jean took out a mobile phone and swiped the screen. "According to her WhatsApp she hasn't been seen since yesterday at just after three in the afternoon."

"Perhaps her phone battery died," Bridge suggested.

"You don't know Kirsty. She would never let that happen. And she carries a power bank at all times. Something has happened to her."

"OK," Bridge said. "I wouldn't worry too much. In the majority of missing persons cases there is usually a perfectly logical explanation for why they've gone missing, and in eighty-six percent of instances they come home, safe and sound within forty-eight hours. A further eight percent are located within a week."

"What about the other six percent?" Jean asked.

"Half of those turn out to have gone missing on purpose," Bridge said. "They have a perfectly good reason for running away."

"And the other half?" Jean said. "The three percent that never show up, what happens to them?"

"Unfortunately, we don't know. It's true that some people are never found, but I don't think your friend is destined to be one of them."

"I'm really worried about her," Jean said.

"You said that you and Kirsty walked to the campus together," Bridge said. "That was definitely the last time you saw her?"

Jean nodded. "The Political Science department is in a different part of the university to the Psychology department."

"Do you know if she had classes all day?"

"She usually does... Hold on, she was giving blood yesterday. She has a rare blood type and she's been donating blood for years."

"Where does this happen?" Bridge said.

"Usually in the refractory, after lunch."

"We'll be able to check if she did keep the appointment to give blood," Bridge said. "It'll be on record. We will get to the bottom of where she's ended up."

"Something bad has happened to her, hasn't it?"

"I very much doubt it," Bridge said. "Like I said, in the majority of missing persons cases they turn up safe and sound. There is no need for you to be worried."

"I've called all the people I can think of," Jean said. "All of her friends, and none of them have any idea where she is."

"What about her family?" Bridge said. "Did you get in touch with them?"

"I didn't think I should worry them just yet. Do you think I should phone her parents?"

"We can do that," Bridge said. "I'll need their contact details, and if you could give me the details of the friends you've already called that would be great too."

"Do you think they could be lying about knowing where she is?"

"I very much doubt it, but we need to speak to them anyway."

"You're taking this seriously, aren't you?" Jean said. "Do you know something? Is there something you're not telling me?"

"Of course not," Bridge said. "We take all missing persons reports extremely seriously."

This was a blatant lie. In reality, a missing persons' report is treated with little more severity than a stolen car. It was a sad truth but with resources as tight as they were, it was simply not possible to thoroughly investigate the disappearance of everyone who was reported missing.

"If you could make a list of Kirsty's friends," Bridge said. "That would be great. And we'll need her parent's contact details too."

"You know something," Jean said. "I know you do."

"I assure you," Bridge said. "This is the general procedure in a missing persons' investigation."

"It's not," Jean argued. "I had a friend whose brother went missing for a week a few years ago. The police did hardly anything about it. The man was twenty-two and they reckoned he was old enough to disappear if chose to. What is it you're not telling me?"

"It's a new initiative. Orders from higher up. We're to make sure that missing persons reports are taken seriously."

Bridge wondered if this lie was apparent on his face. He didn't like deceiving the woman sitting opposite him, but he didn't have much choice.

"Don't worry," he said. "I'm sure Kirsty will turn up soon with a story to tell. You'll probably be laughing about this in a couple of days."

CHAPTER FOURTEEN

"Have we thought of everything?" Whitton asked Smith.
They were driving west on the A64 in the direction of Leeds.
"I think so," he said. "The flights are booked, same with the hotel. I found a really nice place not far from the beach."
"This isn't a holiday, Jason," Whitton reminded him.
"It is sort of. The girls are taken care of – Darren and Lucy are happy to have them next door for a couple of days. Theakston and Fred will have to look after themselves. Darren has promised to feed them and let them in and out. Darren has my car, so he'll be mobile. Your parents will be on hand in case anything goes wrong, so I reckon everything's sorted. Shit..."
"What now?"
"I don't know where Horace Nagel's holiday place is."
"You are kidding me?" Whitton said.
"I'm not," Smith said. "I'm an idiot."
"Are you telling me we're flying to Spain with no idea where we're going?"
"I'll sort it out," Smith said.

He took out his phone and called DI Smyth.
"Where are you?" the DI said.
"On the way to the airport," Smith said. "I need a favour."
"Go on."
"I don't know where Horace Nagel stays when he's in Valencia," Smith said.
"You fool. Didn't you think that might be important before you set off?"
"It slipped my mind," Smith said. "It should be easy enough to track him down. There will be a record of his property somewhere."
"I'll put Baldwin on it."
"Get her to see if he's on social media too. It's a long shot, but he might

have posted something about the place in Spain."

"What time will you be landing in Valencia?"

"Just after seven this evening, Spanish time. There are no direct flights to Valencia from Leeds Bradford and we have a short stop in Amsterdam."

"I'm sure Baldwin will have something for you by then," DI Smyth said.

He went on to tell Smith about the missing university student.

"Do you think it's something to be concerned about?" Smith asked when he was finished.

"Bridge got the impression that the housemate was extremely worried. The young woman doesn't make a habit of not coming home. According to a man we spoke to, Kirsty – that's her name, donated blood at two yesterday afternoon and set off for the house she lives in. She never made it. The house is a ten-minute walk from campus. She doesn't have a boyfriend, and none of her friends have heard from her. It's worrying."

"It is," Smith agreed. "Have you checked the hospitals? It's possible she took a turn for the worse after giving blood."

"It was the first thing we checked. Nothing. And according to the rep at the university responsible for the blood drives, Kirsty has been donating blood since she was sixteen. She has a rare blood type, and her blood is in demand. She's accustomed to giving blood."

"Keep me up to date," Smith said. "And see what you can find out about Horace Nagel's life in Spain."

"What was that all about?" Whitton asked when Smith had ended the call.

She'd turned onto the A1 and they were now heading north.

"Missing student," Smith said. "She gave blood yesterday and never came home."

"Do you think her disappearance could be connected to the woman found by Four Lanes End?"

"I don't know," Smith said. "I sincerely hope not. Did we pack any suncream?"

* * *

DC King was sifting through a pile of missing persons' reports on her desk when DI Smyth came into the room.

"How are you getting on?" he asked.

"These are the all the women who have been reported missing over the past three months," DC King said. "I've ruled out more than half of them, and I'm focusing on the ones who are roughly the same age as the woman found yesterday."

"How many are we talking about?"

"Thirteen, sir."

"Unlucky for some. Did any of them jump out at you?"

"A couple," DC King said.

She'd put the two reports to the side. She picked them up and handed them to DI Smyth.

"Hannah Jones," he read. "And Zoe Granger."

"There isn't much in the reports themselves that can really help us," DC King said. "And Dr Bean couldn't give us much to go on from the postmortem, but we do know that the dead woman had type O positive blood."

"The same as a third of the population," DI Smyth remembered.

"That's right. And we're not in the habit of asking for the blood type of a missing person when a report is filed, but I did some more digging and both Hannah and Zoe have O positive blood."

"How did you get that information? DI Smyth said.

"Creative measures," DC King said.

"Go on."

DC King rubbed her eyes and reached for one of the files. She opened it and gazed at the photograph. She stared at it for quite some time and when she looked across at DI Smyth, he realised that her eyes were bloodshot and teary.

"I recognise her, sir."

The photograph she was referring to was of Zoe Granger.

DI Smyth looked at it too. Zoe was a slim, blond woman with a pretty face and interesting green eyes.

"It's the same woman as the one found in Four Lanes End," DC King said. "Even though there wasn't much left of her, I know it's her."

"You can't possibly ascertain that from what you saw of her yesterday."

"I know, sir," DC King said. "We need to get a sample of her DNA to confirm it, but I know it's her. She deserves to be put to rest properly. Her family needs to know."

The tears that had threatened earlier came now. DC King's eyes were glued to the photograph of the young woman. Zoe Granger's features blurred as the tears flowed but still DC King looked at her. DI Smyth took the file off her and closed it gently.

"I want you to talk to someone," he said. "He's a friend of mine and I think he'll be able to help you."

"Nobody could help *her*, could they?" DC King was sobbing now. "Nobody helped Zoe Granger. Why did someone do that to her? Why?"

DI Smyth placed a hand on her shoulder. "Kerry, I'm going to arrange for someone to drive you home, and I'm going to get a friend of mine to pop round to talk to you. You'll remember him from the *Creed* case."

"The hypnotist?"

"He's also an exceptional psychologist and he'll be able to help you get past this."

"Will this go on my record?" DC King said.

"I don't think that's necessary. Porter isn't even allowed to practice anymore, so let's consider it a friend helping out another friend, shall we?" DC King nodded.

"Go and wait in the canteen," DI Smyth said. "Drink some sweet tea. I'll find someone to take you home."

CHAPTER FIFTEEN

"Kerry's hunch was right," Bridge said and put his phone down on the table. He'd just spoken to Dr Bean at the hospital and the Head of Pathology had given him some information that was definitely relevant to the mystery dead woman.

"According to her medical records," Bridge said. "Zoe Granger had an appendectomy three years ago. Dr Bean found a scar on the right lower side of the abdomen of the woman found by Four Lanes End, and he confirmed that it is evidence of that particular surgery. He didn't pay it much attention during the prelim autopsy – he was more interested in the recent lacerations, but he can confirm that there was an old scar consistent with surgery of that nature."

"When was Zoe reported missing?" DC Moore asked.
"Four days ago," DI Smyth said. "She still lived at home and her parents came in to file a report when she didn't come home from work."
"Was it followed up?" Bridge said.
"As well as it could have been," DI Smyth said. "For what it's worth."
"Can Dr Bean confirm the scar is three years old?" PC Griffin said.
"It's impossible to be that accurate," Bridge said. "But he thinks it could be from that long ago."
"Plenty of people have their appendixes removed," DC Moore pointed out. "It's not conclusive proof that it's her."
"No," DI Smyth said. "It's not, but DNA is, and we'll be asking the parents to provide us with something to compare to a sample taken from the body."
"The poor bastards," Bridge said.
"We won't dwell on that," DI Smyth said. "With Smith and Whitton on their way to Spain and Kerry taking a bit of time off, we're extremely short-

staffed but it can't be helped."

"What's wrong with Kerry?" Baldwin said.

DI Smyth didn't answer the question.

"She'll be back tomorrow," he said instead.

His phone started to ring and the name on the screen caused him to sigh deeply. He let it ring out and soon afterwards a message notification could be heard. DI Smyth opened the message and sighed again. It was from the superintendent and even though it consisted of just three words, DI Smyth knew it was about to make his day even more complicated.

My office, now.

"I'm needed elsewhere," DI Smyth said and stood up.

"Problems?" Bridge asked.

"Something like that. A DNA analysis is going to take time, but in the meantime, I suggest we treat it as a given that the woman found dismembered yesterday is Zoe Granger. Find out everything you can about her. Somebody went to a lot of trouble to do that to her, and I want to know why."

* * *

DI Smyth sensed from the moment he went inside Superintendent Smyth's office that this wasn't going to be pleasant. His uncle looked furious.

"Sit down."

DI Smyth obliged.

"It's been over a week," Superintendent Smyth said. "And I still have no news about my Range Rover. It won't do, Oliver. What are you doing about the carjacking gang?"

"With respect, sir," DI Smyth said. "We have more pressing matters to attend to. The dismembered body of a young woman was found yesterday, and another woman has since gone missing. We've got bigger fish to fry than a group of car thieves."

Superintendent Smyth wasn't listening.

"Am I going to get my car back or not?"

"No," DI Smyth said without thinking. "These people are good. I'm afraid you're going to have to prepare yourself for the worst. Your Range Rover was chopped up for spares very soon after it was stolen."

"And that's all you have to tell me?" Superintendent Smyth said. "My car has been chopped to pieces and you're not even bothering to find out who did it. I want the people responsible to pay the highest price. Do I make myself clear?"

DI Smyth thought back to what Smith had said earlier.

As clear as Uncle Jeremy's garage, now his car is no longer parked in it.

"It's a car, sir," he said. "It's a piece of metal, and it's insured. Like I said, we have more pressing matters to attend to and I need everybody working on that."

"You're just like your father, Oliver," Superintendent Smyth said. "Pig headed. But family or no family I will ask you to remember the chain of command here."

"I'm well aware of the chain of command, sir," DI Smyth said. "This has nothing to do with who has the biggest pips on his uniform – a woman was brutally murdered, and I will not prioritise a gang of car thieves over that."

"Are you disobeying a direct order?"

"I wasn't aware that I was given a direct order. The woman was decapitated. Her arms and legs were amputated, and all of her internal organs were removed. We're dealing with something we've never encountered before, and it needs to be our priority."

"What are you suggesting?" Superintendent Smyth said. "We forget all about a highly advanced team of vehicle thieves?"

"I'm not suggesting anything of the kind. You must agree that a woman's life

is more important than any vehicle, even yours."
Superintendent Smyth's eyes narrowed, and his nephew readied himself for an earful.

It didn't materialise. It was clear that his last comment had gone right over his uncle's head.

"What would you have me do, Oliver?" he said. "What would you do in my position?"

DI Smyth had thought about this, and he decided to take a chance.

"Crime stats, sir."

"Oliver?" Superintendent Smyth's face took on a gormless expression. DI Smyth had seen it many times.

"Your crime stats presentation is just around the corner," he elaborated. "And everybody on my team takes that extremely seriously. We have a deranged killer out there and my gut is telling me that this is just the beginning. The team has never failed to clear up a murder investigation, and we can't afford to let a carjacking ring jeopardise that hundred percent record now."

Superintendent Smyth seemed to be mulling this over. He scratched his nose and nodded.

"Very well. You're quite right, of course, and as you've pointed out the Range Rover was only a car. I've been considering upgrading anyway. No harm done."

For fucks sake, DI Smyth thought.

"We're not disregarding the car thieves," he said. "The investigation is still ongoing, and I'll be assigning some uniforms to it. It all boils down to priorities."

"I suppose I'll have to rely on your judgement then."

"Thank you, sir," DI Smyth said.

"That will be all," his uncle said.

DI Smyth got to his feet and left the office as quickly as he could. As he made his way back to the small conference room, he wondered how on earth he could be related to the public-school idiot who thought he called the shots within York Police. He reckoned it had to be one of those instances where babies were accidentally swapped at birth. It was the only logical explanation.

CHAPTER SIXTEEN

Smith had always hated flying. It wasn't a phobia, as such, but getting on an aeroplane jampacked with complete strangers and ascending thousands of feet into the air had always filled him with trepidation. Perhaps it was because once they were thirty-thousand feet above the ground the only way to go should something go wrong was down. And he didn't relish the thought of perishing beside hundreds of people he didn't know.

The flight from Leeds Bradford to Amsterdam was a short one at just over an hour. No sooner had the Embraer 190 reached cruising altitude an announcement was made, informing the passengers that it was commencing its descent into Schiphol Airport. Fifteen minutes later the plane touched down on the runway and Smith was able to breathe out. He wasn't sure how long he'd been holding his breath, but it took him a while for his breathing to return to normal.

"Are you alright?" Whitton asked him.
"I will be," Smith replied. "When we get off this damn thing and I find a bar with the strongest beer Holland has to offer."
"You do realise that a fear of flying is an irrational one."
"Bullshit," Smith said. "It's perfectly rational. Cramming a bunch of people into a metal box and flinging them thirty thousand feet into the air is not natural."
"Statistically, more people die in road traffic accidents."
"If you say so. I need a beer or two in me before we have to do this again."

They had a two hour wait in Amsterdam before the flight to Valencia, and Smith took full advantage of it. After downing two strong Belgian beers in quick succession, he could feel some of the earlier tension easing off. The waiter informed him that the bar was running a promotion at the moment, and if Smith could manage to drink one more of the 8% proof *Duvel* beers he would qualify for a free T-Shirt.

"Why not?" he said.

"The Valencia flight will be boarding in twenty minutes," Whitton reminded him.

"Plenty of time," Smith decided.

By the time they got on the plane Smith was feeling very relaxed and he was fast asleep as soon as the *fasten seatbelt* lights went out. The T-Shirt he'd earned was in his hand luggage, and Smith didn't know then that whenever he wore it in the future, he would recall the hangover of all hangovers he would experience when he woke up on the aeroplane making its way down to the airport in Valencia. Drinking three bottles of *Duvel* beer in forty-five minutes was not something to be recommended.

Smith had used the airport's free WIFI in Amsterdam and he'd received a message from Baldwin with Horace Nagel's address in Valencia. Smith knew she wouldn't let him down – as long as he'd known Baldwin she'd never failed to impress him. The retired criminal owned an apartment in a complex not far from the hotel Smith had booked. The flight was due to land in Spain at around seven and after retrieving their baggage and getting a taxi to the hotel it would be late so Smith decided to wait until morning to go and pay Horace Nagel a visit.

The plane was fifteen minutes from Valencia when Smith woke with a throbbing headache. His mouth was incredibly dry – it felt like something had zapped every molecule of moisture out of it, and Smith desperately needed some water. He rubbed his eyes and informed Whitton of his predicament.

"Drinking alcohol before flying is not recommended," she said. "They've done research on the subject."

"I'm not asking you to state the bloody obvious," Smith said. "Do we have any water?"

Whitton handed him the bottle she'd been given just after takeoff. It was half full and Smith made short work of it.

"Damn," he said. "What the hell was in that beer?"

"I hope the T-Shirt was worth it."

"Thanks for the sympathy."

The *fasten seatbelts* light came on, there was a sudden jolt, and Smith could sense from the pressure in his ears that they were on their way down to earth. His mouth was crying out for more water, but the cabin crew were already strapped in for landing and he knew he would have to wait until they were on the ground.

The baggage retrieval process was painless enough and Whitton's suitcase was one of the first pieces of luggage to appear on the carousel. Smith had brought along only hand luggage so he left Whitton there while he went to see if he could do something about the drought inside his mouth.

She found him sitting against a wall in the terminal building. A man in uniform was standing over him.

"He's with me," Whitton said to the police officer.

Smith managed to get to his feet. He took a long drink of water.

"Do you need medical assistance?" the officer asked.

He spoke English without any hint of an accent.

"I'll be fine after a good nights' sleep," Smith said.

"Are you here on holiday?"

Smith saw from his name tag that he was Constable Diaz.

"Sort of," Smith told him.

He took out his ID. "DS Smith, and this is DS Whitton."

Constable Diaz looked closely at Smith's warrant card.

"Detective?"

"We're here to speak to someone who lives here in the colder months," Whitton said.

"Is there anything I can help you with?"

"I don't think that will be necessary," Smith said. "But you can point us in the direction of a taxi. We need to get to the hotel."

The Alpina Hotel was a fifteen-minute drive from the airport. Constable Diaz had insisted on giving Smith his card when they said their goodbyes, and Smith had gladly accepted it. It was always useful to have someone who knew the lay of the land on hand to help. He'd worked with Spanish law enforcement in the past and he'd found them to be very cooperative.

The taxi stopped outside the hotel and Smith and Whitton got out. It was just after eight, but the temperatures were still in the low twenties. Smith breathed in and caught a hint of sea air. The Belgian beer hangover still lingered but it was nowhere near as bad as when he'd woken up on the plane.

After checking in Smith and Whitton were told that food was still being served in the restaurant. They decided to freshen up a bit in the room and headed straight back down.

A waitress showed them to a table and handed them a couple of menus. Smith ordered two beers after making sure they weren't particularly strong.

"How's the head?" Whitton asked him.

"Better than it was before," Smith replied. "This is nice – just the two of us. I can't remember the last time we went away together."

"Do you think this Nagel character is going to talk to us?"

"I really don't know," Smith said. "I hope so."

"It's possible that he doesn't know anything about what's going on in York," Whitton said. "What then?"

"I got the impression he knew a lot more than he was letting on. He was the one who brought up *The Workshop* in the first place, and why would he do that if he knew nothing about it?"

"He's a convicted criminal," Whitton said. "And you're a police detective. He could have been stringing you along."

"I don't think he was. Horace Nagel was a sophisticated criminal, but he was old school. He never once caused anyone any harm, and I recall hearing about him being vehemently opposed to violence of any kind. That's how I want to play it – emphasise the extreme violence at play and ask him for his help in preventing any further violence."

CHAPTER SEVENTEEN

"We're not violent people here."

The man's German accent seemed more pronounced now. Kirsty Davies had woken from a dream that consisted of nothing more than white light and it had taken her a moment to remember where she was. She was blissfully unaware that an extensive search was underway. Every available police officer in the city was out looking for her.

"Are you in any pain?"

Kirsty found herself shaking her head.

"That's good, because we wouldn't want the product to spoil."

"What are you going to do with me?" Kirsty said.

"Nothing that will cause you any discomfort."

"Why are you doing this?"

"No more questions. You gave blood yesterday, which is unfortunate. The plasma will have been replenished but the liquid component isn't really the issue, is it?"

"I don't know what you're talking about."

"Yes you do. It will be at least another three to four weeks before your bone marrow produces enough red blood cells to replace the ones lost yesterday. We can risk transfusing before then, but we're not going to do that. There's plenty of time. You're not going anywhere, are you?"

"Tell me why you're doing this," Kirsty begged.

"You don't need to know that."

"I want to go home. Please let me go. I don't know who you are – I haven't seen your face, and I have no idea where I am. Please."

A sound close by caused her to freeze. It sounded like a shutter door being raised.

"Right on time."

The man was further away now.

"Duty calls. You're not the only project on the go right now. Here, at the *Workshop* it never stops. I'll arrange for someone to escort you to your quarters. I'm afraid I'm going to have to help you sleep first."

"Please," Kirsty said. "Please don't do this."

It was like déjà vu. The ice water in her veins seemed to move more quickly this time and Kirsty Davies drifted off to the sound of her heart pounding in her chest.

* * *

"I hope this isn't an inconvenient time."

Porter Klaus smiled at DC King. She'd seemed confused when she saw him standing outside her house. DI Smyth had warned her that the giant German hypnotist would be calling round, but it had clearly slipped her mind.

"Can I come inside?" he asked.

"Of course," DC King said. "You'll have to excuse the mess."

She let him in and led him to the living room. There wasn't really much mess to excuse. There was a coffee cup on the table and that was it. A black cat was asleep on a single-seater chair. It opened one eye when it sensed people inside the room but soon went back to sleep.

"Would you like something to drink?" DC King said.

"No thanks," Porter said. "Oliver asked me to come and talk to you about the woman found by Four Lanes End yesterday. You can tell me to go to hell if you wish."

"I don't know why I reacted like I did. I've seen dead bodies before – plenty of them, but none of them affected me like she did."

"Why do you think that is?"

"I've thought long and hard about it," DC King said. "And I think it's because of what they'd done to her. How could someone do that to another human being?"

"We live in a depraved world. We exist in a society where often cruelty and barbarism is considered acceptable if the price is right."

The cat stretched its legs and hopped off the chair.

"He'll want to go outside," DC King said. "I've been meaning to install a cat flap, but I haven't got round to it. Are you sure you don't want something to drink? I'm going to pop the kettle on anyway."

"Coffee would be great," Porter said. "Black, no sugar."

DC King followed the cat out of the room and returned a few minutes later with two cups of coffee. She handed one of them to Porter.

"Thank you," he said. "How long have you been a police officer?"

"Five years," DC King replied. "I joined up straight after university."

"What did you study?"

"Psychology and Criminology."

"The perfect combination for a police detective. What made you join in the first place?"

"I thought it would be interesting," DC King said. "And I hoped I would be able to make a difference. In retrospect, that's a rather naïve reason, isn't it?"

"Not at all. What you do does make a difference."

"It didn't stop someone doing that to the woman found in Four Lanes End, did it?"

"No," Porter said. "But you will catch the people responsible, and that's what will make the difference."

The cat returned to the room and jumped back up on the chair.

"I envy him," DC King said. "In my next life I want to be a cat. Theirs is a simple life, isn't it?"

"It is," Porter agreed. "I'm going to be straight with you. I don't know whether Oliver told you about my past."

"He mentioned something about you no longer being allowed to practice."

"It's a long, sad story," Porter said. "But yes, I was struck off and I'll never again be able to do the only thing I've ever wanted to do in my life. But that doesn't mean I have to stop helping people. I want to help you, but I need you to be brutally honest with me."

"I am being honest with you?"

Porter nodded. "Tell me what went through your mind when you first saw the dead woman."

"I was confused," DC King said. "It was like it wasn't real – she wasn't real. It was only possible to tell that she was a woman by her breasts. They were the only human aspect on display, and I don't think my brain was able to comprehend it."

"That's understandable."

"It affected everyone who attended the scene," DC King said. "Seasoned forensics technicians were appalled by the brutality on display."

"Human beings as a species are programmed to empathise. It's inbuilt and it's almost impossible to bypass. We're essentially herd animals and we're wired to protect our species for the very survival of that species."

"Tell that to the psychopath who did that to her," DC King said.

A mobile phone started to ring in the kitchen, but DC King made no effort to go and answer it.

"What puzzles me the most," she said. "Is why she was left like that? What purpose did it serve?"

"I'm not sure I understand what you mean?" Porter said.

"Why bother to take her all the way out there?" DC King said. "If you're going to go to all the trouble of chopping off her limbs and her head, and removing her organs, why not just hide what's left of her? It wouldn't have been too difficult to bury a torso. Why put her on display like that?"

"Do you have any theories about that?"

"Either they planned for nature to do its thing with her," DC King said. "Or they wanted her to be found."

"What purpose would that serve?"

"That's what's confusing," DC King said. "We still don't know what they did with her body parts, but whatever it was, surely it would be more beneficial to hide the fact that she was dead. Leaving her on display is a clear indication that they wanted their handiwork noticed, and that's the part I'm struggling to get my head around."

Porter finished his coffee and got to his feet.

"Are you leaving already?" DC King said.

"From what I've gathered," Porter said. "You don't actually need my help."

"The woman's body freaked me out."

"And that's a perfectly natural reaction," Porter said. "But it's clear to me that you've already moved past the horror and the shock, and now your brain is analysing the event from a professional perspective."

"I don't understand."

"You're already considering possible reasons for what was done to her. You're delving into the motivation for why she was mutilated and why she was left on display. While this may not be especially healthy, it's what you do and it's why I believe you're going to move past this quickly. Did what you saw make you angry?"

"It didn't at the time," DC King said. "But I can feel it now."

"That's good. Harness that fury."

He took out a card and placed it on the table.

"Call me if you ever need to talk."

"I don't know if we're going to be able to stop these people," DC King said.

"Hold that thought," Porter said. "Hold onto it tightly."

"How is that going to help?"

"Oliver told me that York CID has a hundred percent clear-up rate in murder investigations. Do you want to know why I think that is?"

"We have an incredible team?" DC King guessed.

"That goes without saying," Porter said. "But it's what makes you so incredible that's important. It all boils down to motivation. It is impossible to beat someone whose motivation is greater than yours. Will you be going to work in the morning?"

DC King nodded. "Definitely."

"I thought you might say that."

CHAPTER EIGHTEEN

When Smith woke the next morning, he was alone in a strange room. He'd fallen asleep as soon as he lay down on the unfamiliar bed and, once again he'd had a dreamless sleep. He wondered where Whitton was. She wasn't in the bed next to him. The sound of the toilet flushing in the ensuite bathroom cleared things up. Smith sat up and rubbed his eyes. He got out of bed and opened the curtains. The hotel they were staying at was three blocks back from the beach and he could just make out the blue of the Mediterranean between the buildings in front of him.

"Wow," Whitton said. "Look at that view. How did you sleep?"
"Like the dead," Smith told her.
"I thought so. You were snoring."
"I don't snore."
"You do," Whitton said. "And you were talking in your sleep."
"What was I saying?"
"It sounded like you were telling Theakston to get off the bed," Whitton said. "You kept repeating, *get down, get down*."
"It must have been that Belgium beer. Remind me not to touch that stuff in a hurry again. What time is it?"
"Just after eight. The weather forecast reckons it's going to get up to twenty-five degrees today."
"It's a shame I didn't bring any shorts," Smith said.
"Probably for the best. We wouldn't want to subject the people of Valencia to your pasty Yorkshire legs. Shall we get some breakfast?"

The dining room in the hotel was quiet. Only a few of the other tables were occupied and Smith wondered why this was. There had been more people last night when they'd eaten there. He would later learn that most of the guests had come and gone. People tended to eat breakfast earlier in Spain.

They helped themselves to some food from the buffet and sat down. A waiter poured them some coffee and left them alone.

"Do you really think he's going to speak to us," Whitton said. "Nagel, I mean?"

"I doubt he's going to welcome us with open arms," Smith said. "He's not the biggest fan of law enforcement, but he's also not a big fan of people who inflict violence – especially where women are concerned. Spain is an hour ahead of York, isn't it?"

"That's right. It's almost half-seven there. What are you thinking?"

"I'm wondering if Chalmers is up yet. He's had more dealings with Horace Nagel than me and he might be able to give me some tips about how to handle him."

"Give him another hour or so," Whitton advised. "He won't thank you for waking him up."

"He'll already be up," Smith decided.

He knew that DCI Chalmers had recently subscribed to WhatsApp so he called him using that.

Chalmers answered after about ten seconds.

"What bloody time do you call this?"

"You're awake then?" Smith said.

"I am now," Chalmers said. "And since when do you phone me on that WhatsApp thing?"

"Me and Whitton are in Spain," Smith said. "I'm using the hotel's Wi-Fi. Can you talk?"

"What the hell are you doing in Spain? I thought you were in the middle of a nasty murder case."

"That's why we're here. Do you remember Horace Nagel?"

"There's a blast from the past," Chalmers said. "What about him?"

"That's what we're doing here," Smith said. "He's got a place in Valencia where he goes to escape the cold in York. I've spoken to him once, but not for long. What can you tell me about him?"

"Nagel?" Chalmers said. "He was probably involved in half of the serious crime in the city in the eighties and nineties. He did a ten year stretch in Full Sutton if I recall, but he got away with a hell of a lot more than that."

"He never used violence in the robberies, did he?"

"Not once. And that was his downfall."

"What do you mean?"

"He was caught because of a jumped-up security guard," Chalmers said. "It was at one of the big banks in the city. Nagel and his team were carrying fake weapons, and the guard tried his luck. I wasn't involved but I heard that it was something legends are made of. The security guard got a bit carried away with his fists, and Nagel and the three blokes he was working with lay down and took it on the chin. It was before the days of CCTV, unfortunately. That would have been something to see. Why are you so interested in an old crock like Nagel?"

"He mentioned something that caught my attention," Smith said. "He said he'd heard a rumour about some kind of workshop where it's not car parts that are being chopped up. I got the impression that he knows a lot more about it than he let on."

"Good luck with that. Nagel might be old school, but he's never been our biggest fan."

"What else can you tell me about him?" Smith asked.

"He was born in Holland," Chalmers said. "I think he's in his seventies now."

"Seventy-two," Smith said.

"He was way ahead of his time. Saw opportunities before most of the competition did."

"How do we get him to talk to us?"

"A bottle of single malt might soften him up a bit," Chalmers said. "I didn't have much to do with him, but I can make a few calls for you. What time were you planning on paying him a visit?"

"As soon as possible."

"Hold off a bit. I think Barry Coleman was at Full Sutton when Nagel was sent there. He'll know more than me."

"I appreciate it," Smith said.

"When are you coming back to York?"

"Tomorrow. It's a fleeting visit. Has something happened?"

"Not that I'm aware of. There's been no more decapitated women anyway. I'll see what Barry has to say, and I'll get back to you."

Smith thanked him and ended the call. He filled Whitton in on the gist of the conversation.

"I'm starting to wonder if this is a waste of time," she said. "How long is it going to take for Chalmers to get back to you?"

"As long as it takes," Smith said.

"And what do you suggest we do in the meantime, twiddle our thumbs?"

"Beach," Smith said.

"What?"

"We're in Spain," Smith said. "The sun is shining – let's go for a walk on the beach."

CHAPTER NINETEEN

"The bad news is," DI Smyth said. "There have been no new developments overnight. But that could also be construed as good news. Kirsty Davies has still not been located."

"How is that good news?" DC Moore said.

"It means there's a chance that she's still alive," Bridge said.

"We've retraced Miss Davies' movements on Monday," DI Smyth said.

"Kirsty left the university campus after giving blood at roughly three in the afternoon. She rents a house half a mile away from there and she usually walks the same route. We've got the CCTV footage from a few of the businesses along the way, and one of them can put her close to the sports village at 15:12. The owner of the bakery on Kimberlow Lane also remembers someone matching her description coming into the shop at about that time."

"What about her phone records?" DC King said.

"The last time she used the phone ties in with the time she was seen close to the sports village," DI Smyth said.

"The woman who came in to report her missing said the last WhatsApp she sent was just after three," Bridge said.

DI Smyth approached the huge map on the wall at the back of the room. He drew a circle around the bakery and then he drew another one around a location in the middle of Farndale Avenue a few hundred metres to the north.

"This is where she was last seen." He tapped the pen on the bakery. "And this is where she was going."

It was the house Kirsty lived in, in Farndale Avenue.

"She was taken somewhere between those two locations," Bridge said.

"It looks like she was," DI Smyth said.

"What else is there on the way?" DC Moore said.

"There's the petrol station on Hull Road," Bridge said. "And then it's all residential properties."

"If she was abducted," DC King said. "I'd say it's more likely she was taken before she made it to the residential area."

"Surely it would be less risky to grab her where the streets aren't so busy," DC Moore said.

"We're not going to waste time speculating on that," DI Smyth decided. "Any other thoughts?"

The room fell silent for a moment. DC King was the first to speak. "What if she knew the person who took her?"

"It's not unheard of," DI Smyth said. "We've already spoken to the people on the list of friends we managed to get, but we could be missing someone."

"Can I say something?" It was DC Moore.

"This is not primary school, Harry," DI Smyth told him. "You do not have to raise your hand to ask a question."

"Sorry, sir. We're working on the assumption that she was abducted. What if we've got the wrong end of the stick?"

"I don't think we have," Bridge said. "Everybody who knows Kirsty has told us the same thing – this is highly out of character for her. She's been missing for almost two days, and nobody has heard a peep out of her."

"With respect, Sarge," DC Moore said. "It has happened before. Straight A student shacks up with a boyfriend nobody knows about. The friends and family all tell us the same story – this is not like her, but then the missing woman turns up after spending a couple of weeks away with some bloke."

"No," DC King said. "This is not one of those instances."

"How can you be so sure?"

"I just know."

"And in light of the dead woman from Four Lanes End," Bridge said. "We have to take this seriously."

"Moving on to that," DI Smyth said. "We know that she had type O blood. According to the missing persons' database two women around the same age with that blood type were reported missing in the past few months. Kerry."

"Hannah Jones and Zoe Granger, sir."

"We've spoken to the parents of the two women," DI Smyth said. "And it didn't take long to rule out Hannah Jones. The photograph we got from her mother and father depicts a large woman. Hannah is tall and she weighs close to fifteen stone."

"How long has she been missing?" DC Moore said.

"Five weeks," DI Smyth.

"Is it possible she's lost weight in that time?"

"Not that much weight. The photo was a recent one, Harry. Hannah was a large woman with big breasts. The woman found on Monday was slight with small breasts."

"What did the other woman's parents have to say?" Bridge said.

"They were justifiably distraught," DI Smyth said. "What parent wouldn't be when they're asked to provide something for DNA comparison purposes?"

"What did we tell them?" Bridge said.

"We didn't give them the details, of course," DI Smyth said. "But people are not stupid. When a couple of police officers knock on your door and tell you something like that, you're going to fear the worst, even when you're assured it's simply to rule your daughter out."

"How long will it take to get a result?" DC Moore said.

"We'll probably have a confirmation, one way or the other by tomorrow."

"It's her," DC King said. "It's Zoe Granger. I saw her. I know it's her."

"And we'll be looking very closely at Miss Granger while we wait for the test results," DI Smyth said. "As of now we know very little about her. She was single and she worked part-time in a supermarket in Tang Hall. That's about all we know at this stage. The uniforms who went to see her parents got a list of her friends from them, and we'll work our way through that list during the course of the day. We'll also be taking a close look at her phone records. It's possible there's a perfectly reasonable explanation for her disappearance."

"How long has she been missing?" Bridge said.

"Eight days."

"It's her," DC King said. "It's Zoe Granger."

CHAPTER TWENTY

Smith and Whitton were in a taxi heading south towards Beniparrell. It was just before noon and the sun was directly overhead. Horace Nagel owned an apartment in a small complex at the marina at Port de Catarroja and, according to the GPS on the dashboard it was two kilometres away.

Smith's phone had beeped six times in quick succession when they got back to the hotel after their stroll on the beach. There was no Wi-Fi signal away from the hotel and Smith had neglected to consider this when he suggested a walk.

There were three messages from DI Smyth. All of them were asking for the update Smith had promised to send twice a day. He typed a short message to DI Smyth informing him that they were meeting Horace Nagel soon. He would have more to report then. There was a message from Darren telling him that everything was fine at home. Smith replied to this one with a thumbs-up. A WhatsApp from his insurance company was informing him that his car insurance was a month overdue. Smith made a mental note to sort that out when he got back to York. He'd let Darren borrow his car while he was away and, technically the car wasn't allowed to be on the road, but Smith didn't think it was anything to worry about.

The final message was from Chalmers.
Answer your bloody phone.
That one had made Smith smile. He'd phoned the DCI as soon as he could, and Chalmers had told him about something Barry Coleman remembered. The custodial manager of Full Sutton recalled that Horace Nagel had struck up a close friendship with another inmate during his time in prison. Boris Jackson was in for a triple murder, and he was still incarcerated. Chalmers suggested to Smith that he should tell Horace Nagel that Jackson sends his regards. Smith wondered why a confirmed pacifist like Nagel would befriend

a triple murderer, but Chalmers had told him that Barry Coleman reckoned the two men were close during their time inside and Smith decided it was worth a shot.

They passed by the bird sanctuary and Smith gazed out at the sea beyond it. He could understand why Horace Nagel chose to spend the colder months here instead of back in York. There wasn't a cloud in the sky and the thermometer on the dash told him it was twenty-five degrees outside. The Spanish weather forecast was clearly more accurate than it was back in Yorkshire. Smith glanced down at the plastic bag by his feet. The bottle of Laphroaig had set him back a pretty penny in the boutique shop by the hotel, and he hoped it was worth it.

After paying the driver Smith and Whitton were informed that they would have to make their way to the security office by the boom gate preventing unauthorized access to the apartment complex. Smith hoped the security guard wasn't going to give them any problems. They had their warrant cards, but he didn't think the English police had any jurisdiction in Spain.

The security officer spotted them first. A tall man in a green uniform intercepted them before they'd reached the boom gate and said something in Spanish.

"Do you speak English?" Smith asked him.

"Of course," he replied.

The expression on his face suggested that Smith had asked a really stupid question.

"This is private property," he said. "You need to leave."

Smith had half-expected this. He took out his ID and handed it over.

"York," the security guard read and studied Smith's face.

"We're here to see one of the residents here," Whitton explained. "Horace Nagel."

"Mr Nagel doesn't like to be disturbed."

"I appreciate that," Smith said. "But we really need his help. He's not in any trouble."

The security guarded nodded. "I can speak to him, but if Mr Nagel doesn't want to talk to you, you'll have to leave."

Smith held up the plastic bag. "Tell him I brought whisky."

He watched as the man returned to the security office. He was inside for a few minutes then he emerged and walked back over to Smith and Whitton.

"Mr Nagel says he will see you. He lives in number 7. Go through the gate and follow the road round to the end."

Smith could feel the relief flooding his system.

"Thank you. We really appreciate it."

"I have an uncle in Yorkshire. In Leeds. Paulo Lopez – perhaps you know him."

"It's a big county," Smith said. "Thank you for your assistance."

* * *

Kirsty Davies sensed that she wasn't alone. When she'd woken a few hours earlier her head had been extremely foggy. Whatever drug they'd given her had caused her vision to blur and her ears had been temporarily blocked, but now her senses were clearing, and she could detect a sound she hadn't been aware of before. Someone else was inside the room and they were breathing heavily.

Kirsty turned her head to locate the source of the sound, and something clicked in her neck. She raised a hand to it and realised that she was free to move her arms. Earlier, she'd been bound to the chair but now her shackles were gone.

There was a bed a couple of metres from hers, and there was a man lying on it. When Kirsty looked closer, she could see the tubes that were attached to his arms. He had an oxygen mask over his mouth, and that's what Kirsty had been able to hear earlier. The mask was attached to the face using two strips of adhesive tape. The man's chest was rising and falling, and she wondered what was wrong with him.

Then something occurred to her – something that caused her own breathing to quicken. Was this some kind of hospital? It that was the case, what was she doing there? She recalled snippets of the conversation with the man with the German accent. What had he told her?
We wouldn't want the product to spoil.
What had he meant by that?
You are in possession of a very valuable commodity.
That part was even more baffling.

She pulled back the sheets and slid her legs over the edge of the bed. Her limbs were tingling but she could still manoeuvre them. She took hold of the cannula inserted into her wrist and yanked it out. She dared to stand up and her vision went black for a few seconds. After a few deep breaths her sight returned, and she took a closer look at the unconscious man in the other bed. He didn't look very old. His eyes were closed and the mask over his mouth covered a lot of his face, but Kirsty could see that his skin was pale and smooth. Once more, she wondered what was wrong with him.

She didn't get the chance to dwell on it. There was a loud click, and Kirsty heard the door open. Two figures dressed in white came into the room. Kirsty couldn't tell if they were men or women – they had surgical masks over their noses and mouths and they were both wearing peculiar goggles.

"Please return to your bed," the shorter of the two said.
Kirsty recognised the voice. It was the man with the German accent.
"Where am I?" she asked.
"Return to your bed please," the other one said.
It was definitely a woman, and her accent was local.

"If you do not do as we ask," the man said. "We will have to force you, and you won't like it if we do that."

"You can't keep me here," Kirsty said. "I want to go home. People will be missing me."

"Of course," the man said, and sighed.

He glanced at the patient on the bed and headed back to the door. Kirsty heard voices and soon afterwards two more people entered the room. They too were wearing facemasks and the same weird goggles. Without warning they took hold of an arm each and frog-marched Kirsty back to the bed. A fresh cannula was inserted, and the injection was quick.

As the frozen sedative invaded Kirsty's bloodstream again, she caught four words spoken with a German accent.

Prepare him for surgery.

CHAPTER TWENTY ONE

Horace Nagel's expression was difficult to read when he opened the door to Smith and Whitton. The ex-criminal looked them up and down and if Smith didn't know any better he would swear he looked mildly amused.
"You've come a long way."
"We really need to speak to you," Smith said after introducing him to Whitton. "I brought you something."
He handed Horace the bag. He took out the bottle and his smile broadened.
"York Police's budget seems to have improved."
"It came out of my own pocket," Smith said. "And it wasn't cheap."
"Single malt isn't, here in Spain. I suppose you'd better come in. You'll have to excuse me for a moment while I finish my crossword."

He went inside and Smith and Whitton followed him in. Smith watched as Horace sat in front of a laptop and scratched his nose.
"There's always one or two that stump me."
"One or two what?" Smith said.
"Clues. I like to complete the online Guardian cryptic crossword every day. It's good to keep the old brain active, but I think this one is going to beat me."
"I've never been much good with cryptic clues," Smith said.
"What's the clue?" Whitton asked.
"Old civil orders to detain criminal set," Horace read. "Producing toxin. Second letter *S*, fourth letter *E* and last letter also *S*."
"I would have thought a clue like that would be right up your alley," Smith said.
Horace ignored him.
"Any ideas?" he said to Whitton.
"Asbestos," she said without thinking.

Horace looked at the screen and shook his head.

"Of course. What a fool I am. That means the final answer is *Tiptoes*. Thank you, dear – you're welcome back anytime. Let's chat now."

He suggested they talk in the garden. The apartment was smaller than Smith expected it to be. He imagined a criminal mastermind living in a luxury villa with a sparkling pool. This was more like a two-bedroomed ground floor flat with a view. Horace Nagel read his mind.

"It's not what you imagined, is it?"

"Not really," Smith said.

"Some of the ex-pat criminal fraternity here own palaces further down the coast. What's the point in that? I don't want full-time maids and full-time security detail. I'm a simple man and this suits me fine. When the sun finally makes an appearance in York I can lock up and go without having to worry about securing the place."

He opened up a double patio door and gestured for them to go outside. "Take a seat. Can I offer you something to drink? I'm afraid I don't drink whisky when the sun is high in the sky, so the Laphroaig will have to wait for another time."

"Of course," Smith said. "Anything cold and wet."

Horace walked away in the direction of the kitchen and came outside a couple of minutes later.

"Emily will make us some fresh lemonade."

"Is Emily your wife?" Whitton asked.

"She's the help. She works two days a week, and today is one of those days. What is it you want from me?"

Smith didn't get the chance to tell him. A stocky woman with black hair came outside with a tray of lemonade. She nodded to Whitton and scowled at Smith.

"She seems like a barrel of laughs," Smith said when she'd returned to the house.

"She's suspicious of strangers," Horace said. "it's not a bad trait to possess. Help yourself to the lemonade."

"When I spoke to you on Monday," Smith said. "You mentioned something that grabbed my attention."

He took a sip of lemonade.

"Some kind of workshop," he added.

"It's just something I heard about," Horace said.

"Can you tell us some more about it?" Whitton asked.

"The rumour is, there's a place in the city where a chop shop is being run. And it's not motor vehicles that are being taken apart."

"A meat market," Smith said. "Your words."

"To put it crudely, yes. But the people involved are far from crude. I don't know the details, but it seems they're highly organised, and their influence is far-reaching."

"Could you elaborate on that?" Whitton asked.

"I've said too much already. I've already told you, I'm not a snitch. Will there be anything else? I have a sailing trip arranged for three this afternoon."

"I thought all the ex-pats came here for the golf," Smith said.

"A ridiculous pastime. You're thinking of the English. We Dutch are a seafaring nation."

"We need your help, Horace," Smith said. "Someone out there is subjecting women to unspeakable violence, and we have to stop them." This wasn't strictly true. So far, they only had one victim, but Smith's words seemed to bring about a change in Horace Nagel's demeanour. Smith decided to try and keep the momentum going.

"I'm not going to go into details," he said. "You don't want to hear how badly disfigured the victims were when they were found. Let's just say there were seasoned forensics technicians who were traumatised by what they saw. Tell us some more about *The Workshop*."

"Please," Whitton said. "We need your help."

"I've told you all I know," Horace said. "I'm sorry for these women. As you know, I deplore violence of any kind, but all I've heard about The *Workshop* is what I've already spoken about. I wish you a safe trip back to England."

Smith was running out of options. Horace was ushering them out the door when he remembered what Chalmers had told him about the man Horace had befriended in prison.

"Barry Coleman asked me to let you know that Boris Jackson sends his regards."

This stopped Horace in his tracks.

"Boris?"

"You were inside together I believe?" Smith said.

"A long time ago. Good Lord, is he still alive?"

"Alive and well," Smith said.

"Boris was one of the good ones in that place."

"He was sentenced to life without parole for triple murder," Smith reminded him. "I wouldn't have thought you'd be friends with a man like that. I thought you detested violence."

"It's a long story," Horace said. "Sometimes things are not as they seem."

"We're here in Valencia until tomorrow," Smith said. "We can meet up again when you're back from sailing."

"Please, Horace," Whitton said. "You might be able to help us find out who's behind *The* Workshop."

"I can't help you," Horace said.

"I never expected you to be a man who would sit back and allow this level of violence to continue, Horace," Smith said.

"I didn't mean it like that. If you would shut up for a second and let me finish, I'll explain."

"I'm all ears," Smith said.

"How are your sea legs?" Horace said.

"Not great," Smith admitted.

"The breeze isn't forecast to get up too much this afternoon. The man who owns the boat might just be able to help you find what you're looking for."

"You want me to go out on a boat?"

"Do you want some answers?"

"We'll be there," Whitton said. "Just tell us when and where."

CHAPTER TWENTY TWO

The temperature in York was exactly twenty degrees colder than it was in Valencia and that was one of the reasons why it would take Dr Bean and his team longer than usual to determine the time of death of the man waiting by the railway tracks in Overton. The dead man was soon to be discovered by an unfortunate dogwalker, but the recent cold snap in the city was going to cause confusion, and it was something the team working on the investigation could really do without.

The poor soul who was destined to stumble on something she would never be able to erase from her mind was Valerie Powell and she and her Border Collie were heading north not far from Nether Poppleton.

Valerie zipped up her coat further to shut out the biting wind that was blowing across the open ground surrounding the river. Jock was walking to heel, and he was oblivious to the cold. They followed the path that skirted the river, and they were nearing the tracks when Jock stopped. He sniffed the air a few times and Valerie saw that the fur on his back was standing straight up.

"What is it, boy?"

Jock sniffed the air again and started to tug on the lead. Valerie suspected there was a fox or a rabbit close by and she resisted the urge to let him off to go and explore. He was still a youngster, and she didn't want to risk him running towards the road to their right.

They carried on past the small lake and they were about fifty metres from the railway lines when Valerie felt an almighty tug on the lead and Jack was gone. She watched as he darted in the direction of the tracks.

"Jock," she shouted.

The Border Collie wasn't listening. He carried on running and stopped right next to the track. He was too far away for Valerie to see exactly what he was doing but his body language told her that he'd found something very interesting.

* * *

The call came in ten minutes later, and it took PC Baldwin a further five minutes to get the woman on the other end of the line to calm down enough to tell her what had happened. Grant Webber and his team were parked up on Overton Road within the hour and from there it was a five-minute trek across a field to the railway tracks.

Webber, Billie Jones and Pete Richards walked in silence. The woman who had called the switchboard hadn't been able to give them a very clear picture of what they were heading towards, but Baldwin knew it was bad from Valerie Powell's reaction. She told Webber as much.

Webber crossed the railway track first with Billie Jones close behind him and Pete Richards bringing up the rear. Webber stopped as soon as he stepped off the track. He held a hand in the air to indicate to Billie and Pete that they were to go no further. Webber hadn't got a good look at the figure on the ground, but he'd registered enough to tell him they were going to be here for a very long time.

He told Billie and Pete to put on their protective clothing and he made a start on doing the same.

"What did you see?" Billie asked.

"It's bad," Webber said. "Prepare yourself."

Billie nodded. Pete Richards looked like a man with a fear of heights who was about to skydive for the first time. His eyes were staring straight ahead at nothing in particular and his breathing was rapid.

Webber placed a hand on his shoulder. "Calm yourself. This is nothing you haven't done before."

The condition of the man was nowhere near as bad as the woman found by Four Lanes End. His head was still attached to his neck and all his limbs were accounted for, but Webber would later explain that it was this that actually made what had been done to the rest of him worse. There was little doubt that this corpse was human, but where his stomach and chest once were was now a jagged mass of skin, muscle and pulpy flesh. His ribcage was exposed and most of the bones had been broken.

Webber focused on the man's face. He didn't think he was very old – perhaps early to mid-twenties and his skin was unusually smooth. His muscle tone suggested he kept himself in shape and Webber wondered if he liked to frequent the gym. This was a young man in his prime, and his life had been cut short.

"I want the area from here to the Shipton Road sealed off." He got down to business.

"Do you think the people who brought him here came from that direction?" Pete asked.

Webber nodded. "It's logical. Otherwise, they would have to drag him across the train tracks and I doubt they will have done that. You can't get a car this far into the field, so they will have had to come the last part on foot. Get hold of some uniforms. I want this done now and I want them to make the cordon a wide one. I don't care how much time it adds to our day – I want these bastards caught. They will have left something behind when they brought him here, and I will not risk missing it."

Billie didn't have to be told how to do her job. She set up her camera and proceeded to take photo after photo of the body and the surrounding area. It was bitterly cold now but none of them seemed to be feeling it. The early afternoon sun was fighting a losing battle with the clouds that were forming overhead. No rain was forecast but all three forensic technicians knew that meant nothing in Yorkshire.

"Do you think it's the same people?" Billie asked the question that all three of them were considering.

"Yes," Webber said. "It's the same people. Why bother bringing him all the way out here? Why not just dispose of him somewhere hidden away?"

Billie wasn't listening. Her attention was caught by something on the dead man's neck. The first sirens could be heard in the distance.

"What is it?" Webber said.

"It's the same people," Billie said.

She carried on snapping away, focusing on the man's neck. There, just below his left ear was a raised welt. The man had been branded with an @ sign.

CHAPTER TWENTY THREE

Smith and Whitton arrived at the marina twenty minutes early. The Valencia Mar was a massive harbour, housing sail and power vessels of all shapes and sizes. It was coming to the end of the summer season but there was still a lot of activity on the water. Boats were coming and going in the marina, a few people were carrying out maintenance on their vessels and passenger ferries were bring people back and forth to the port.

Smith was unaware that another body had been found in York. He didn't know that a young man had been discovered by the railway lines with most of his chest destroyed. He would find out about it later, and he would curse his decision to travel to Spain when he was desperately needed back in York.

Horace Nagel had given them the name of the yacht his friend owned but Smith realised they would need a bit of assistance in locating the vessel. There were hundreds of boats in the marina and he didn't know where to start looking. The security guard manning the gate pointed them in the right direction. The boat was a ninety-foot yacht called *Serenity*, and it was berthed at the far side of the marina, close to the harbour entrance.

Horace was already there when they stopped next to the vessel. He waved a hello and told them to step aboard. *Serenity* was in immaculate condition. She was an Oyster 885 and if Smith knew anything about boats he would be aware that the price of the vessel he and Whitton had been invited aboard was somewhere in the region of 5 million Euros. It had luxury accommodation for eight guests and the cost of chartering an Oyster 885 was around fifty-thousand Euros per week.

Even though Smith wasn't aware of the money on display here, he still felt out of his depth. This was a different world to his – this was the world of the rich and famous and it made him feel slightly uncomfortable.

A few people were milling around on the deck. Two men were fiddling with something on the mainsail. A woman was removing covers from the cushions on the foredeck and another woman was doing the same in the cockpit. None of them spoke and they seemed to be taking their work very seriously.

"Make yourself comfortable at the stern," Horace signalled to the spacious cockpit.

Smith shuffled to the back of the boat, his hand gripping the safety rail the whole time.

Horace laughed. "Bit of a landlubber, are we?"

"Boats are not natural," Smith said.

"Relax," Horace said. "She's one of the most stable yachts you'll ever sail on."

Whitton was clearly more at ease. She stepped down into the cockpit and took a seat on the starboard side.

"Where's your friend?" she asked. "The man who owns the boat?"

"He's taking a nap down below," Horace said. "He'll be up shortly. He's not well."

Smith managed to make himself comfortable opposite Whitton and he took in his surroundings. He had to admit that the Oyster 885 was unlike any boat he'd ever been on. The teak deck was well maintained, and the paintwork was immaculate. Two huge wheels were attached to sturdy pedestals on either side of the vessel. A control panel that resembled something from a Boeing 747 took up most of the fore section of the cockpit and a wide stairwell led down below decks. Smith wondered what it was like down there.

"Could I get you something to drink?" a man's voice broke Smith's reverie.

He looked up to see a young, tanned man standing over him. His accent was Australian.

"What have you got?" Smith asked him.

"Anything you like. Water, wine, whisky. Or beer."

"I'll have a beer thanks," Smith said.

Whitton asked for one too.

Horace Nagel took a seat next to Smith.

"What do you think?"

"Wow," Smith said. "I don't want to know how much this thing cost."

"The running costs alone run into forty thousand a month," Horace said. "She has a permanent crew of six – the marina fees are extortionate, and the maintenance costs are horrendous, but she pays for herself during the summer season."

"Is she for charter?" Whitton asked.

"She is," Horace said. "If you have a spare fifty grand, you and seven friends can enjoy absolute luxury for a week."

"I have to tell you," Smith said. "I have no idea how to sail."

"Call yourself an Australian?"

"I was a surfer, not a sailor."

"Don't worry," Horace said. "You won't have to lift a finger. The crew are well-trained and they're also well paid. They will do everything. We'll be setting sail soon."

"Tell us about the owner of the boat," Whitton said. "Who is he?"

"You'll meet him soon enough," Horace said. "Paddy is quite a character."

"Paddy?" Smith repeated.

"You might know him as Patrick Carroll."

Smith was suddenly wide awake. Patrick Carroll was definitely a name he'd heard before. It was before his time, but Carroll was someone you did not want to cross a few decades ago. He was a notorious gangster and something of a philanthropist in his day. Smith recalled that he had a reputation for being a bit of a paradox. He was a known kingpin in the underworld, but he also had a heart of gold.

The Australian steward returned with the drinks and the sound of coughing could be heard down below. The coughing fit continued for quite some time and then Smith caught a whiff of cigarette smoke. The deck crew stopped what they were doing and all of them stood stock still as though they were standing to attention. *Smith's* attention was caught by movement in the companionway. Two skeletal hands were gripping the handrail. A figure emerged and another coughing fit ensued.

Patrick Carroll didn't look like a hardened criminal. The man who'd once controlled most of the organised crime in Yorkshire now resembled nothing more than a skeleton. His face was tanned but the skin looked like it had shrunk onto the bones. A cigarette was dangling from two thin lips. He reached the top step and was helped to the cockpit by one of the crew.
"Thank you Lizzie," he said to her.
The Irish accent was still very obvious.

"Paddy," Horace said. "Sleep well?"
"I woke up," Paddy said. "Which is always a good thing."
He laughed and started to cough again. He removed the cigarette from his mouth and looked at it as though he couldn't remember it being there.
"Damn thing has gone out."
Smith took out his lighter and handed it to him.
Patrick looked him in the eye and gave Smith what he thought must be a smile.
He took the lighter and relit the cigarette. "Much obliged."
"Paddy," Horace said. "This is Jason and Erica. They're two detectives from York and they've come a long way to have a chat with you."
"Later," Patrick said. "Let's get this girl sailing first."

The crew sprung to life. The captain stood behind the control panel and with a touch of a button the engines came to life. Two deckhands made short work of the mooring lines, and another touch of a button activated the bow thrusters and the yacht slowly reversed away from the jetty. Five minutes later, they were free of the confines of the harbour and the ninety-foot yacht increased her speed and headed out to the open sea.

CHAPTER TWENTY FOUR

Dr Kenny Bean thought he'd seen everything in his time at the hospital. The experienced pathologist had come across things so horrific it would shock a seasoned soldier, but the young man on the metal table in front of him was something he didn't think he would ever forget.

The man had been in pristine physical shape when he was still alive, and Dr Bean concluded that he was no stranger to sports. His shoulders were broad, and his muscle definition suggested he spent a lot of time participating in physical activity. His legs were muscular and hairless. His arms were also smooth, and Dr Bean couldn't understand why this was. He outlined his confusion with his assistant.

"I think he might be a swimmer," Sarah Monk suggested.
"A swimmer?" Dr Bean repeated.
"My cousin used to swim for the county," Sarah said. "He was really good – very competitive, and he used to shave his legs before a competition."
"What on earth for?"
"He reckoned it made him more streamlined through the water," Sarah said. "A lot of swimmers do it – cyclists too."
"You learn something new every day."
"The branding on the neck is baffling," Sarah said.
"How so?" Dr Bean said.
"It's the same brand as the one on the woman we examined, but the damage inflicted to the man is vastly different. If it's the same people responsible, why did they do that to her and not to him?"
"We'll leave questions like that up to the people who are paid to find the answers, Sarah," Dr Bean said. "What else can you ascertain about this poor soul?"

An initial examination had determined that the man's chest had been sliced open from top to bottom. The ribcage had been exposed and subsequently cracked open. The heart and the lungs had been removed but the liver and the kidneys were still where they were supposed to be. This was also different to the woman they'd examined. All of her vital organs were taken.

"I think this was done in a hurry," Sarah decided.

"I'm inclined to agree with you," Dr Bean said. "One deep laceration to expose the ribcage and a clamp in the correct place to open up the chest cavity. The lungs and the heart were not surgically removed – they were ripped out, and what does that tell us?"

"They'd be useless as transplant organs."

"Precisely. The mitral valve and the tricuspid valve were left behind, rendering the heart permanently unable to function. Why remove them in such a way as to leave them with no monetary value?"

Sarah's silence told him she didn't have an explanation for this.

"Time of death is going to be tricky to ascertain," Dr Bean continued. "The temperatures over the past twenty-four hours haven't risen above seven degrees."

"No rigor or liver mortis," Sarah said. "Even taking the outside temperature into consideration, he hasn't been dead long."

"We'll be examining the remaining organs more closely," Dr Bean said. "And that ought to give us a more accurate time of death, but I agree with you – I don't think he's been dead longer than twelve hours."

"I've taken samples for a tox examination, and I'll be doing that when we've finished here."

"This is interesting," Dr Beam was looking at something on the man's face.

"What are those marks on his cheeks?" Sarah had spotted it too.

On each side of the man's face were identical red stripes. They were roughly an inch wide, and they extended from the cheekbones to the ears.

"It looks like the result of adhesive bandages or something similar," Dr Bean said.

"Possibly a respirator mask?" Sarah speculated.

"I suppose we'll never know."

"Are we going to close him up?"

"Whoever did this to him has made that virtually impossible," Dr Bean said. "No, we've got enough to get through without attempting a pointless task."

* * *

Darren Lewis arrived at his parents' house to find a police car in the road outside. He parked Smith's Sierra behind it and went to see what was going on. He hoped it wasn't anything serious. His first thoughts turned to Lucy. He took out his phone and called her number. After a brief conversation he learned that she was safe and sound at home with Laura and Fran. Darren wondered if something had happened to Smith or Whitton. He went inside the house to find out.

It was PC Griffin and PC Greg Hill. Darren sighed – he'd had a run in with the former officer earlier in the year. He'd been stopped by the piggy-eyed PC and arrested for driving without a license.

"What are the police doing here?" he asked.

His parents were sitting in the living room. The two police officers were sitting opposite them.

"Just a routine visit," PC Hill said. "I think everything's cleared up now."

"We're still going to need to corroborate Mr Lewis's alleged story about where he was on Monday night," PC Griffin added.

"It's not an alleged story," Frankie Lewis said. "I was here all night. My wife has already confirmed it."

"I've come to learn that an alibi provided by a spouse is often unreliable," PC Griffin said.

"Why are you asking my dad where he was?" Darren asked.

"Like I said," PC Hill said. "It's just routine. I think we can leave it at that."

"I don't think we can," PC Griffin disagreed. "Mr Lewis, you are a known felon – you have a record, and your name is on a list of persons of interest to us in an ongoing enquiry."

"That was a long time ago," Frankie said. "I've kept my nose clean for years."

"You know what they say about leopards," PC Griffin said.

"I promise you," Frankie said. "I had nothing to do with the recent carjackings."

"I wasn't aware that we'd gone into the specifics about why we're here," PC Griffin said. "You seem to know an awful lot about something you claim to have had nothing to do with."

"The vehicle thefts have been all over the news," PC Hill reminded him.

"That's right," Frankie said. "It's not a crime to keep abreast of the news, is it?"

"We'll be keeping an eye on you," PC Griffin said.

Frankie Lewis didn't even bother to comment on this.

"I'd better be getting back," Darren said. "I just came by to drop off a few of Andy's things. How is he?"

"He's fine, love," his mother, Jenny said. "He's sleeping now."

"We won't take up any more of your time," PC Hill said.

He stood up to indicate to PC Griffin that it wasn't up for debate.

Darren left them to it. He went outside - made his way back to Smith's car and got inside. He put on his seatbelt and checked the road around him. He turned the key in the ignition, the car lurched forwards and there was a terrible crunch as Smith's Sierra slammed into the back of the parked police car. Darren had left the car in gear and he'd forgotten to disengage it when he'd started it up.

CHAPTER TWENTY FIVE

The two police officers were out of the house in an instant. Frankie and Jenny Lewis were close behind them. Darren's parents followed PC Griffin and PC Hill to the scene of the accident outside. Darren was already standing on the road next to Smith's car and he was inspecting the damage.

"That was a really stupid thing to do."

It was PC Griffin. He too was examining the back of the police car. The distance between it and Smith's Sierra wasn't great and it could have been a lot worse. The rear bumper was cracked but it was still attached to the police car. The left taillight had been smashed, and apart from that the damage was mostly cosmetic. Smith's car had come away pretty much unscathed. The middle of the left headlight had a slight crack in it and the paintwork was chipped, but Darren knew that it was easily fixed.

PC Griffin didn't share Darren's optimism. He assessed the damage and shook his head.

"It was an accident," Darren told him.

"Of course it was," PC Griffin said. "Seconds after we've finished questioning your father, you decide to retaliate by damaging police property. That is a very serious offence."

"It was an accident," Darren said once more. "I forgot to take the car out of gear when I started her up. I'm sorry."

"It's a bit late for apologies, son."

Frankie Lewis walked over and took a look at the back of the police car. "That's nothing that can't be sorted out quickly. Our Gary can have that looking like new in an afternoon."

"I don't think so," PC Griffin said. "This will have to be documented. A report will need to be filed, and a charge of criminal damage will be brought against your son."

"Accidents happen," PC Hill joined in. "Like Mr Lewis said, the damage is minimal. The car is still drivable, and I don't think we need to take this any further than getting the insurance companies involved."

"I'll have to get their details from Mr Smith," Darren said.

"You do that."

"I don't think we can let this drop, Greg," PC Griffin said. "How do we know he didn't do it on purpose?"

"Because we've all done it," PC Hill said. "I've done it. It's an easy mistake to make – you leave the car in gear and turn the key without depressing the clutch. The young lad didn't do it on purpose."

"I assume you have a license?" PC Griffin wasn't giving up so easily.

Darren took out his driving license and handed it to him.

"A report will have to be filed, regardless," PC Griffin said. "We'll need DS Smith's insurance details for that report."

Smith was hundreds of miles away, enjoying a leisurely sail on a superyacht, and he was blissfully unaware of the headache that was coming his way. His insurance premiums hadn't been paid for over a month, and this lapse was going to come back to bite him on the backside.

* * *

The Oyster 885 was cruising along at a leisurely eight knots under mainsail alone. The engines had been switched off and the only sound was the wake as the hull ploughed through the water. Smith had to admit that he was actually enjoying himself. He'd never been a big fan of boats, but he could get used to the luxury on offer right now.

Lunch had been served on deck, and Smith was halfway through his third beer. Patrick Carroll hadn't spoken a word since they left the marina, but the Irish gangster had managed to smoke four cigarettes since setting off.

After the lunch plates were cleared away, Smith decided it was time to bring up the reason they were there. Patrick Carroll was nursing a tumbler of whiskey. He'd hardly touched it since it was brought to him.

"Are you sick?" Smith asked him.

Patrick nodded. "The Big C. It's in my lungs and it's going to be the death of me."

"You have lung cancer?" Whitton said. "I'm sorry."

"It is what it is," Patrick said.

"And you still smoke?"

"Why the hell not? The docs advised me not to, but they also advised me to get treatment, so it just goes to show what little they know."

"You refused treatment?" Smith said.

"It took me less than the time it takes to smoke a cigarette to make up my mind," Patrick said. "I was given the numbers. I could have an extra six months to look forward to if I did what they told me to do. Six months of hospital appointments and drugs that make me feel like I want to die anyway. Where's the logic in that?"

Smith had to agree with him. He had a valid point.

"I've got morphine for the pain," Patrick said. "And I'm not afraid of the end. It's one of life's inevitabilities, isn't it? That and taxes."

"What do you know of taxes?" Horace said.

"You got me there, but we won't discuss that in front of a couple of coppers. What do you want from me?"

This question was addressed to Smith.

Patrick Carroll had been open with him since they'd been invited on board, so Smith decided to tell him the truth.

"What do you know about *The Workshop*?"

Patrick lit another cigarette but made no effort to smoke it.

"It's not what you think it is."

"It rarely is," Smith mused.

"Tell me what you know so far?"

Smith told him everything that had happened in York in the past few days. He told him about the torso of the woman, and he told him about his fears about the missing university student. He didn't leave anything out.

"You need to suspend disbelief right now," Patrick said and drained his whiskey in one quick gulp. "Listen to what I have to tell you but push all rational thoughts from your mind. Can you do that?"

Smith reckoned he could. He told Patrick as much.

"I'm a dead man walking for talking to you about this," the Irishman said. "But you'll probably understand that that's nothing new to me. I'm already living on borrowed time."

"Why are you agreeing to this?" Whitton wondered. "I didn't get the impression that you were the kind of man who would talk to the police."

"Because what they're doing is wrong," Patrick told her. "What these bastards are doing is very wrong."

CHAPTER TWENTY SIX

DI Smyth rubbed his eyes and stared at the huge map of the city on the wall in the small conference room. The locations that had been circled began to blur, and he took a step back. He wasn't quite sure what he was hoping to achieve from this exercise. Did he expect something to jump out at him and hit him in the face? Something so obvious he would curse himself for not noticing it earlier? He didn't think so. It was just after four in the afternoon, and he'd scheduled a briefing for quarter past, but he needed some time alone to go through the events once more without any distractions.

The body of the woman they suspected was Zoe Granger had been dumped in a field close to the caravan park in Four Lanes End. There were two access roads to that area and the perpetrator could have come from either direction. DI Smyth decided that the location was chosen carefully. It was far enough from any human habitation to ensure the people involved weren't caught in the act, but it was also a popular spot for hikers and day visitors and it was likely the body would be found quickly.

DI Smyth's eyes now focused on another sinister circle on the map. This one was by the train tracks north of Nether Poppleton. Grant Webber was convinced that the dead man had been brought to the tracks from the direction of Shipton Road. DI Smyth traced the probable route with his finger and stopped fifty metres from the road.

He turned his attention back to the first victim and something occurred to him. Both victims were dumped a stone's throw from a caravan park. The woman they believed to be Zoe Granger was found not far from the Ashfield Park and the man was discovered very close to the Grantchester Caravan and Camping Park. DI Smyth knew that this was something they needed to look more closely at.

"What are you looking at, sir?"

It was DC King. She and Baldwin had come into the room together.

"Both bodies were dumped within close proximity of camping grounds, Kerry?" DI Smyth said.

"Do you think that's significant?" Baldwin asked.

"I don't know. It could be."

"Bridge was supposed to arrange for some uniforms to check out the Ashfield Caravan Park," DC King said. "I'm not sure if he did."

Bridge and DC Moore came in shortly afterwards. They were in high spirits, and they appeared to be sharing a joke.

"Are you going to let the rest of us in on it?" DI Smyth said.

"Darren Lewis drove Smith's car into the back of one of our patrol cars," Bridge said.

"You're kidding?" DC King said. "Is he alright?"

"It was just a bit of a bumper bash," DC Moore said. "Hardly any damage, but it was Griffin who was driving the police car."

"God help us all," DC King said.

"He wasn't in it," Bridge said. "But he was still pissed off. He reckoned that Darren did it on purpose."

"Why would he do that?" DC King asked.

"Because the car just happened to be parked outside Darren's parents' house. Griffin and PC Hill were there to interrogate his dad about the recent carjackings. Griffin wanted to arrest Darren for criminal damage. That bloke needs a good talking to."

"Is Darren in trouble?" Baldwin said.

"Not really. He's got his license now, and Smith's insurance will cover the damage to the police car."

"As much as I'd like to carry on this conversation," DI Smyth said. "We have more important matters to discuss. While I was taking a look at the locations where the bodies were found I realised they're both a short distance away from camping grounds."

"Could be important," DC Moore decided.

"Bridge," DI Smyth said. "Did you manage to check out the park by Four Lanes End?"

"There's hardly anybody there," Bridge said. "The man and woman who found the first body and another couple. It's late September and the place will be closing for the winter soon."

"But the park is still open to the public?"

Bridge nodded. "It is, but only two of the sites are occupied."

"I want to take another look at the place. The same goes for the Grantchester Caravan and Camping Park. That one is close to the road, not far from where the man was found this morning."

"Do you think these people could be operating out of campsites?" DC King said.

"It's possible," DI Smyth said. "We need to find out what else is at those campsites."

"There are a few static sites," Bridge remembered. "And ablution blocks, but I don't remember seeing anything that could pass as a workshop. Besides, bringing bodies to and fro would arouse suspicion. The places are still operational and there's always someone there overseeing the running of them."

"I want them checked out anyway," DI Smyth said. "It's a connection that needs following up."

"There's still no news about Kirsty Davies," Baldwin said. "Her phone hasn't been used since three on Monday afternoon, and there have been no sightings of her."

"Her family are worried sick," DC King said. "As are her housemates. This is so out of character for her. She's never disappeared without telling someone where she's going before."

"I still think it's too early to presume she's another victim of these *Workshop* people," DC Moore said.

"It's been two days, Harry," DI Smyth said. "She's been missing for over forty-eight hours. That is something we cannot overlook."

"How close are we to getting a confirmation that the first victim is Zoe Granger?" Bridge asked.

"We'll know for sure tomorrow," DI Smyth said.

"Can't they speed things up a bit?" DC King said. "Her parents must be frantic."

"They're going as fast as they can. It's getting late, but I want those campsites checked out before you call it a day. Bridge, you and Harry can take the one in Grantchester, and Kerry and Baldwin can have a look at the one in Four Lanes End."

"What exactly are we looking for, sir?" Baldwin said.

"Anything that seems out of place at a campsite. Outbuildings that are locked – that sort of thing."

"Have you heard anything from Smith and Whitton?" Bridge said.

"As a matter of fact, I haven't," DI Smyth said. "He promised to keep me in the loop, and he hasn't kept that promise. I sincerely hope that this trip to Spain hasn't been a complete waste of time."

CHAPTER TWENTY SEVEN

Sailing vessel *Serenity* was currently under anchor about ten nautical miles off the coast of Valencia. Patrick Carroll had instructed the crew to drop the sail and lower the anchor. He'd then told them to take a break below decks. He didn't want any of them to overhear what he was about to discuss with Smith and Whitton. Horace Nagel had also made himself scarce, and Smith wasn't quite sure why. The Dutchman was taking a nap in the master cabin. Patrick had made sure Smith and Whitton were suitably fed and there were six beers in a bucket of ice on the table in front of them.

"A few years ago, a shocking series of events came to my attention," Patrick said. "I'd recently retired, but I was still reasonably well informed. Innocent people were being abducted and killed for their internal organs." Smith had made short work of four beers, but he was suddenly stone cold sober. He remembered the case well. How could he forget it – it almost cost him his life.

"The Enigma," he said.
Partick observed him with watery eyes. "You're aware of it then?"
"I was involved in the investigation," Smith told him. "It started down in Cornwall – in a place called Trotterdown. A boat drifted in during the night and nobody had any idea where it came from. There were dead bodies on board and all of them had had their vital organs removed."
"I didn't know about the boat down in Cornwall," Patrick said. "But I did get wind of the boat that was found just off the north-east coast."
"That one was also called *The Enigma*," Smith remembered. "We followed the trail, and it led us to an extremely dangerous crime lord."

He didn't elaborate on this. He didn't want to dwell on it. The man responsible for the illegal organ trade was a man he hadn't thought about for a long time and he wanted to keep it that way.

"Are you suggesting that someone else has copied this particular business model?" he said instead.

"No," Patrick said. "This isn't about illegal human organ trafficking – this is something much worse."

"What can be worse than the human organ trade?" Whitton asked.

"Let me explain a few things to you," Patrick said. "Help yourselves to the beer. The ice won't stay frozen forever."

Smith obliged. He cracked open two bottles and handed one to Whitton.

"As you were involved in the *Enigma* case," Patrick carried on. "You'll understand the nature of that business. It's complicated, and it's tricky to get away with. In order for organs to be preserved for transplant purposes, there have to be measures in place to keep them healthy. They need to be removed properly, and they need to be kept under certain conditions. And they have to be delivered to their recipients quickly. This is not only costly – it's extremely risky."

"What are these people doing with the body parts?" Smith asked the million-dollar question.

"The victims are being murdered to order," Patrick said. "It's not dissimilar to your carjackers. They get a list of vehicle parts - these vehicles are stolen, chopped up and shipped out to the clients for a price. The same thing is happening with the body parts."

Smith wasn't sure he wanted to hear the answer to his next question, but he had to ask it.

"What are these people doing with the body parts?"

"That all depends on the client," Patrick said. "There always has been and there always will be a black market for all things unobtainable. Trade in ivory has been outlawed for decades yet there are still Chinese fat-cats who are able to get their hands on it. There is nothing that cannot be bought if money is no object. What you're looking at right now is a shrewd bunch of businessmen who have cottoned on to this."

Patrick still hadn't answered Smith's question.

"What are they doing with the body parts?" he asked again.

"All sorts," Patrick said. "It's not a one size fits all business model. Let me give you a few examples. A wealthy Chinese man wants the head of a beautiful woman – all he needs to do is ask how much."

"That's disgusting," Whitton said.

"It's happening," Patrick said. "He keeps it preserved in a jar in his private collection, and nobody is any the wiser. He shows it to a friend of his, and this friend has heard about the healing powers of drinking the powdered heart and lungs of a healthy athlete. It's delivered to him, and he slips a few spoons of it into his tea. It's as macabre as it gets, but if you've got enough money, you can get hold of anything. Some of them like to drink blood. They believe it can offer them eternal life, but it has to be the right type of blood. The people operating *The Workshop* can make it happen. We're talking about a multi-million-dollar enterprise here."

Smith was finding it hard to take all this in, and he was feeling a bit ill. Patrick Carroll had asked him to suspend disbelief, but he didn't think he'd have to suspend it to such an extent that he was expected to consider that something he'd described really happened in the twenty-first century. He couldn't believe that innocent people were being slaughtered to pander to the whims of faceless billionaires.

He decided to focus on something else.

"How are these people getting the products out of the country?"

He cringed at his choice of word. *Product*s sounded rather innocuous under the circumstances.

"How do you think?" Patrick said. "Under cover of darkness with armed guards on hand."

He stopped there to gauge Smith's reaction. Smith didn't rise to it.

"They're using a front, aren't they?"

"You're smart," Patrick said.

"A legitimate export operation," Smith elaborated. "They'll have all the necessary paperwork in order. They'll make sure all their licenses are up to date, and they'll probably be someone reputable. Someone nobody would even think to look into."

Patrick looked at Smith and the expression on his face was somewhat disconcerting. The Irish gangster's eyes took on a resigned aspect to them and Smith didn't like it one bit. He got the impression that their conversation was almost over.

"Do you know who these people are?" he asked even though he was certain what Patrick's reply was going to be.

"Of course not. I only know what I've told you because I was offered an *in* a while ago."

"Someone approached you?" Whitton said.

"Not *someone*," Patrick said. "That's not how these people operate. It's all done discreetly with no risk of repercussions. A friend of a friend of a friend, and so on. We'd better think about heading back in. I'm feeling rather weary."

"Is there anything you can tell us about these people that might give us an idea of where they're operating out of?" Smith said.

Patrick reached over and pressed a red button on the control panel.

"The crew will be back on deck soon."

"We have no idea where they're running their workshop from," Smith said.

"If what you've told us is true then we now know why they're doing this, but we still don't know where they're working from."

"I don't know," Patrick said.

"You must have some idea," Whitton said. "You seem to know an awful lot about these people."

"I don't know where *The Workshop* is," Patrick said. "But I have my suspicions about some people who could fit the bill."

"Help us," Smith said. "We really need your help."

"If I were you, I would take a close look at a company who operate under the name *Artemis Trading*."

"Who are they?" Smith said.

"*Artemis Trading*," Patrick said. "That's all I'm going to tell you."

The hatch on the companionway was removed and the crew of *Serenity* began making their way back on deck.

CHAPTER TWENTY EIGHT

Bridge parked his car next to the office at the Grantchester campsite and he and DC Moore got out.
Bridge rubbed his hands together. "It's bloody freezing."
"Too cold for camping," DC Moore said. "Why would anyone want to come here at this time of year?"
"Let's go and see if there's anyone in the office."

They made their way inside and both detectives were glad for the warmth within. The campsite's reception building also housed a small shop and the shelves were stacked with the basics people might need while camping. A small fridge contained milk, some canned drinks and not much else. There was nobody inside and it didn't appear that anyone was manning the reception desk.

Bridge walked over to it and noticed that there was a door leading off from behind the desk.
"Hello," he shouted. "Anyone here?"
Soon afterwards a middle-aged man appeared in the doorway. He looked Bridge up and down and Bridge got the impression he was nervous. He looked like a man who'd been caught doing something he shouldn't.
"Can I help you gentlemen?"
Bridge took out his ID. "DS Bridge, and this is DC Moore. And you are?"
"Bob."
"Bob what?" Bridge said.
"Just Bob. All the campers call me Bob. What do you want?"
"Are you the manager here?" DC Moore said.
"Manager," Bob said. "Groundsman, all round gopher. Can I help you with something? Only I was just about to lock up."
"It's not yet five," Bridge said.

Bob nodded to the door. "Reception is open from eight until five. Opening hours are clearly stated on the door."

"We'll try not to keep you too long then," DC Moore said.

"How many guests are staying here at the moment?" Bridge said.

"I'll have to check the book."

"Could you do that please?" DC Moore said.

The guest book was on the desk right in front of him, and when Bob opened it, Bridge wondered why he'd tried to draw the process out. When he informed them how many campers were present on the site he was also confused. According to the guest book, two of the static caravans were occupied and a man on his own had pitched a tent. That was it. Currently there were only five people there.

"We're going to need to talk to the campers," Bridge said. "And we'd like to take a look around the campsite."

"What for?" Bob said. "What's going on?"

"Just a routine check," DC Moore said.

"I'm supposed to be watching my boy play football," Bob said. "He's in goal for the school and this is the first match of the season."

"What time is the match?" Bridge asked.

"Half-five. If I don't make it the wife won't let me hear the end of it."

"OK," Bridge said. "I'm sure we can do what we need to do without you here. Just a few questions before you go."

Bob looked at his watch. "Can you make it quick?"

"How long have you worked here?"

"Six years. The pay isn't great, but I like the job. I'm mostly outside."

"There's only one road in and out of the campsite, isn't there?" DC Moore said.

"That's right. Stripe Lane."

"And you'd notice if any vehicles came past here and carried on in the direction of the railway tracks?"

"That depends where I was on the grounds."

"Do you remember any vehicles passing by in the last day or so?" Bridge said. "

"Not that I recall. There's no reason to go any further than the campsite. There's nowt further along but the railway lines."

"We won't keep you any longer," Bridge said. "Enjoy your son's football match."

Bob shrugged his shoulders. "Between you, me, and the doorpost it'll probably be his last. Butter fingers doesn't even begin to describe it. But you have to support your kids, don't you?"

"I wouldn't know about that."

"Do I need to let Mr Garden know you're here?" Bob asked. "He's the owner of the campsite."

"That won't be necessary," DC Moore said.

It didn't take Bridge and DC Moore very long to find the people who were staying at the campsite, and it took them even less time to realise that none of them were going to be able to tell them anything useful. The man camping alone had just returned from a long hike and he'd set off at first light. He hadn't seen or heard any vehicles close to the campsite apart from the cars belonging to the occupants of the static caravans.

The couple in the first caravan were happy to talk to them but neither of them had remembered any vehicles passing by either. The occupants of the last caravan were more reluctant to open up, but Bridge got the impression that they didn't like talking to anybody, and when the woman informed them that she and her partner had recently returned from a four-month retreat in Peru Bridge decided they were wasting their time.

The caravan park wasn't very big, and a tour of the grounds could be done in less than ten minutes. There were two ablution blocks – one for men and one for women, but after checking both Bridge and DC Moore couldn't see anything out of the ordinary about them.

"There's nothing here that could be used as any kind of workshop," DC Moore said. "I think we're barking up the wrong tree."

Bridge agreed with him. An operation as advanced as the *Workshop* would have to be carried out somewhere remote and even though the campsite fitted the bill for that, there were people here, and he didn't think anybody would be able to chop up human bodies without anyone suspecting something.

They were making their way back to the car when Bridge spotted someone walking in their direction. It was the man who was here on his own.

"Sorry to trouble you," he said.

"Is everything OK?" Bridge said.

"Something occurred to me. When I was heading out this morning there was this van."

"Where was this?" DC Moore said.

"I was making my way out of the campsite, and when I turned left onto the road the van passed me."

"Which direction was if heading in?" Bridge asked.

"Towards the campsite."

"Had you seen it before? Perhaps it belonged to one of the other campers."

"They've all got cars."

"What time was this?" DC Moore said.

"Just before it got light. About half-six."

"Can you describe the van?" Bridge said.

"Sorry, I didn't pay much attention to it. It was just an ordinary white Transit van."

CHAPTER TWENTY NINE

Smith stepped off the boat and onto the jetty. Whitton and Horace Nagel were next to disembark. Patrick Carroll remained on board the Oyster 885. He'd told them that he was going to spend the next few days on the boat. The accommodation aboard the superyacht rivalled that of any luxury hotel and Smith could understand his decision to remain on board.

He was still trying to process what the Irishman had told him. At any other time, he would find Patrick's revelations ridiculous, but in light of what the woman by Four Lanes End had been subjected to Smith had to consider it. He decided he would head straight back to the hotel and use the free Wi-Fi there to bring DI Smyth up to date. Smith and Whitton would be back in York tomorrow but by the time they landed in Leeds Bradford it would be late afternoon, and Smith wanted the team to see what they could find out about Artemis Trading in the meantime. Patrick Carroll had seemed convinced they were involved somehow.

"What does your evening look like?" Horace asked.
They were at the exit gate of the marina.
"I need to make a few calls," Smith said. "Your friend gave us something to look into."
"Why did he even agree to talk to us?" Whitton said. "I never expected him to."
"Paddy is something of an enigma," Horace said. "Back in his day he wouldn't have given you the time of day – me neither, but people change as they come to appreciate the concept of their own mortality."
"He told us that he's a dead man walking for speaking to us," Smith remembered. "What about you? Are you not concerned for your safety?"
"I'll take my chances. I have my own protection – people who look out for

me behind the scenes. I'd like to invite you and your lovely wife out to supper."

"We've abused your hospitality enough already," Whitton said.

"Nonsense. I know this place that does the best seafood in Spain."

"OK," Smith said. "But dinner is on us."

"You'll regret saying that," Horace said. "You'll regret saying that when you see the prices on the menu."

Smith and Whitton got a taxi back to the Alpina Hotel. It was just after seven, but it was still warm. They'd agreed to meet Horace Nagel at the restaurant at half-eight. It would give Smith enough time to call DI Smyth with a long overdue update. If Patrick Carroll thought Artemis Trading was something to consider Smith had to take it seriously.

He paid the taxi driver, and they made their way inside the hotel. Smith retrieved the key from reception and the man behind the desk informed him that someone had tried to get hold of him. Smith assumed it was DI Smyth. He'd given him the contact details of the hotel and as far as he was aware he was the only person who knew where they were staying. Smith thanked the receptionist and he and Whitton headed up to their room.

While Whitton took a shower Smith took out his phone and called DI Smyth. He answered immediately.

"Where have you been?"

"Gathering information," Smith said.

"I tried to get hold of you at the hotel four times."

"We were out on a boat," Smith told him.

"You're not there on holiday, Smith."

"It was work. Horace Nagel introduced us to an old friend of his. Patrick Carroll – I don't know if you've heard of him."

"The name rings a bell," DI Smyth said.

"He was a big-time crook in his day. Irishman. He's retired now, but he still knows things. Any new developments in the investigation?"

"The body of a man was found earlier," DI Smyth said. "His chest had been opened up and his lungs and heart were removed."

"What about the kidneys and liver?"

"Still where they should be. No ID on the man, but it looks like it's the same people. Both victims were left close to campsites, and we've checked them out."

"Anything?"

"Not really," DI Smyth said. "A camper remembered seeing a white Ford Transit van on the road close to the campsite in the early hours of this morning, but he couldn't give us any more than that. Do you know how many white vans there are on the road?"

"Too many to check all of them," Smith said. "Any news on the missing student?"

"She's still missing, and it's a cause for concern. We did learn something about her though. She has a rare blood type – AB negative. Apparently fewer than one percent of the population has that blood type."

It was as if a light had been switched on inside Smith's head – an extremely bright light, and everything became clear in an instant. He recalled a snippet of the conversation with Patrick Carroll.

Some of them like to drink blood. They believe it can offer them eternal life, but it has to be the right type of blood.

"Kirsty Davies is still alive, boss."

"She's been missing for more than two days," DI Smyth said. "Nobody has seen or heard from her in that time."

"They took her because of her rare blood type," Smith said. "They're going to keep her alive so they can extract that blood."

"You're not making any sense."

"Hear me out," Smith said. "This is going to sound extremely farfetched but I think I know what's happening. Patrick Carroll told us some things that could be written into the script of a horror movie. There are people out there – rich people, and they like to collect macabre trophies. These sick bastards will pay top dollar for human body parts."

The line went quiet for a while.

"Are you still there, boss?" Smith asked.

"Still here," DI Smyth confirmed. "I'm trying to process this. What else did your Irishman tell you?"

"He gave me some disturbing information. He said there are billionaires who will pay a lot of money for the head of a pretty woman. Once they have it, they'll display it in a case in a private exhibition. Others believe they will become stronger by consuming the lungs and heart of an athlete, and some think that drinking a certain blood type will offer them eternal life. We've got our motive."

"Good Lord," DI Smyth said. "I believe you could be onto something."

"I know I am."

"The first victim had her head, and her limbs amputated. And her organs were also removed. We're certain it's Zoe Granger and the photographs of her depict a stunningly beautiful young woman. The man found earlier today had no ID on him but, according to Dr Bean he was extremely athletic. Kenny's assistant suspected that he could have been a competitive swimmer."

"And only his lungs and heart were taken?" Smith said.

"Correct. And now we have Kirsty Davies. Her rare blood type is probably the reason she was abducted. I'm inclined to agree with you – Miss Davies is much more valuable to these people if she's kept alive."

"Patrick Carroll gave us the name of a business we should look into," Smith said. "Artemis Trading. He's not a hundred percent sure, but he reckons this is something they might be involved in."

"Artemis Trading?" DI Smyth said.

"You need to do some digging. I think the body parts are being shipped out legitimately. They're being exported by a reputable company that nobody would even suspect."

"We'll look into them tomorrow. Do you have anything else to report?"

"Nothing, boss," Smith said. "We need to get to the bottom of this."

"That goes without saying."

"We need to do it quickly. Kirsty Davies is still out there somewhere. Somewhere in York she's being held against her will so these bastards can milk her like a fucking cow."

CHAPTER THIRTY

Kirsty Davies had never felt so frightened in her life. The episode with the underground bunker paled into insignificance compared to her current predicament. She was seven years old, and she and her family were on holiday in Germany. They'd visited a theme park and one of the attractions was the bunker system where small children could crawl underground. Kirsty's brother thought it would be funny to scare her by blocking the exit of one of the bunkers with a wooden crate. Kirsty hadn't been amused. Her seven-year-old mind had conjured up a nightmare where she was destined to remain trapped underground forever. The claustrophobia that followed was debilitating, and Kirsty still suffered from it, years later.

The dread she'd experienced in that bunker was a walk in the park when she compared it to where she was now. She didn't know who the people who'd taken her were, but one thing was crystal clear – they were keeping her alive for a reason. The man who had been in the room earlier wasn't there when Kirsty regained consciousness, and she didn't think she would ever see him again.

In his place was a woman who didn't look much older than a schoolgirl. The mask over her mouth and nose was identical to the one the man had been wearing, and Kirsty felt a sudden urge to help her.
"Can you hear me?"
The young woman didn't respond. Her eyes remained closed and there was no indication that she'd heard Kirsty's voice.
"I'm Kirsty. I'm going to try and help you."
   "Don't waste your time."
The voice came from somewhere inside the room, but apart from Kirsty and the mystery girl there was nobody else there.

"She's beyond helping."
Kirsty looked around and spotted the speaker in the top left-hand corner.
"You're the special one, Kirsty. You're the golden child – Miss one in a hundred and sixty-seven."
Kirsty froze. That was what the man in the van had called her. Luke, she remembered. But the voice she'd heard on the speaker wasn't his – this was the man with the German accent.

"You can't keep me locked up," Kirsty screamed at the speaker.
The silence that followed was more unsettling than the man's voice.
"Let me out of here."
The door of the room opened with a click and two of the masked strangers came in. Once again, they had the odd goggles over their eyes.
"Please return to the bed," one of them said.
Kirsty recognised his voice. It was Luke, the man who'd given her a lift in the van.
"You're going to give blood," the other one said.
It was a woman.
"I can't," Kirsty told her. "I donated blood on Monday."
"That's unfortunate," Luke said. "And the two units we're about to extract will render you extremely weak, but the client has upped the price she's willing to pay, and business is business."

Two more people came into the room and Kirsty had no option but to allow them to escort her to the bed. She was so accustomed to what happened next, she didn't even flinch as the cuff was wrapped around her arm and the needle was inserted. Soon she felt the familiar sensation of the blood being extracted. The bag next to the bed was full to its 450ml capacity in less than ten minutes.

"One more."
Luke's voice. Kirsty was already feeling giddy, and they were only halfway

there. The bag of blood was removed and replaced with a fresh one. As the process was repeated Kirsty could feel her eyelids becoming heavy.

"It's nothing personal," Luke told her. "We really didn't want to do this, but in the end it all comes down to supply and demand."

* * *

"Supply and demand," Smith said.

He'd showered and now he was getting dressed.

"Supply and fucking demand. People are being butchered, and it's all about money. I really hate money."

"Calm down," Whitton said.

"How can I calm down when a woman is being held captive because of a rare blood type?" Smith said. "How can I calm down when there are people in my city who think they have the right to trade in something that doesn't belong to them? This world really has gone insane. Can you believe this is actually happening?"

"We live in a sick world," Whitton said. "You've said it yourself a million times, but it's our job to catch the sick bastards and make them pay. We'll catch them. They can't get away with this for much longer."

"I don't know about that. Money talks, and these fuckers have a lot of it."

Whitton's phone started to ring, and she was glad of the distraction. She hated it when Smith got in these maudlin moods. The screen told her that it was Lucy.

"Hi there," she said. "How are things?"

"Is Dad there with you?" Lucy asked.

"Of course he's here with me," Whitton said. "Hold on... I'll put you on speaker."

"No..."

It was too late. Whitton had already activated the speaker.

"What's wrong?" Smith asked.

"Is it Laura or Fran?" Whitton said. "Has something happened to one of the girls?"
"They're fine," Lucy said. "It's Darren. He went round to his parents' house to drop a few things off for Andrew and two police officers were there."
"What were they doing there?" Smith said.
"They wanted to talk to Darren's dad about the carjacking thing. That's not why I'm phoning. Darren had a slight accident in your car."
"What did he do?" Smith said. "Is the car alright?"
"What my husband meant to ask is whether Darren is alright," Whitton said.
"He wasn't hurt," Lucy said. "He left the car in gear and it lunged forwards when he started it. There wasn't much damage, but unfortunately, the car he hit was the police car."
"Fuck," Smith said.
"PC Griffin wanted to arrest him," Lucy carried on. "For wilful damage of police property or something, but the other officer persuaded him not to."
"Griffin is a prick," Smith said.
"Anyway, they need to file a report, so they'll need your insurance details."
"Fuck," Smith said once more.
"It'll be fine," Whitton said. "Nobody was hurt, and the insurance company will sort out the damage."
"I'm not insured," Smith told her.

CHAPTER THIRTY ONE

"What do you mean you're not insured?"
Whitton was furious. She and Smith were on their way to the restaurant Horace Nagel had recommended. As luck would have it, it was only half a mile from their hotel, so they decided to go there on foot. It was after eight, but the streets were busy and Smith deduced that people liked to eat late in Spain.

"Well?" Whitton said. "What's the story with the insurance? I thought you'd got it sorted out."
"I might have let it lapse," Smith said.
He took out his cigarettes and lit one.
"I got a message the other day reminding me that it's overdue and I didn't get round to sorting it out."
"You bloody idiot," Whitton said. "You do know that driving without insurance is illegal."
"Of course I know."
"You're a police officer, Jason," Whitton said. "You bloody idiot."
"I wasn't to know that Darren would drive into the back of a fucking police car. Why did it have to be Griffin? That bastard isn't going to let this lie."
"Darren could get points on his license for this." Whitton wasn't quite finished yet. "He's only just got that license."
"Perhaps he should have thought about that before he rammed into the back of a patrol car," Smith said. "Can we change the subject? There's nothing we can do about it now. I'll smooth things over when we get back to York."

The rest of the walk passed in silence and Smith was glad. The sun was getting ready to turn in for the night but, according to a thermometer underneath a clock in the plaza, the temperature was twenty-one degrees.

Smith wondered why Horace Nagel had invited them out to eat. Did he have an ulterior motive?

The restaurant was situated right in the heart of the plaza. Horace was already there when they arrived. The Dutchman was sitting at a table for three outside. He stood up when he spotted Smith and Whitton, said a few words to a waiter and beckoned with his hands for them to come and join him.

He checked his watch. "Right on time. Take a seat."

"This place looks fancy," Whitton said.

"It is essential to book in advance," Horace told her. "You can't just come in from the street and expect to get a table."

"How did you manage to get a booking at such short notice?" Smith asked.

"Because I own the place. Well, I'm a part owner – sixty percent."

"You still keep yourself busy then?"

"I'm more of a silent partner. What would you like to drink? I have beer brought in from Belgium if you're that way inclined."

Smith wasn't. He still hadn't forgotten the headache from the last Belgium beer he sampled. He decided to play it safe and stick to the milder Spanish brew.

The waiter brought the drinks and handed out two menus. Smith opened one and realised two things straight away. He had no idea what was on offer – all of the names of the dishes were in Spanish. The second thing he registered was there were no prices on half of the items on the menu. He asked Horace why this was.

"A lot of the dishes on the menu are subject to availability," Horace explained. "We use the services of local fishermen and sometimes we're not able to source certain fish. It's all about supply and demand."

Supply and demand, Smith thought.

He was beginning to detest that term.

Horace recommended a dish called *Bacalao a la Vizcaina* which he loosely translated as grilled cod in a tomato-based sauce.
"The chef here cooks it with potatoes, onions and hard-boiled eggs," he added.
"I'll give that a go," Whitton said. "It sounds delicious."
"I don't suppose they do a steak and ale pie here?" Smith said.
Whitton shook her head.
"I'm kidding," Smith said. "I'll try the cod thing too."
Horace put the order in and shortly afterwards the waiter returned with what appeared to be a small seafood platter.
"A tapas appetizer," Horace explained. "Grilled baby octopus, garlic shrimp and calamari rings. Dig in, as you English say."
Smith helped himself to some calamari. He dipped it in the tartar sauce and popped it in his mouth.
"Why did you invite us here this evening?" he asked when he'd finished chewing.
"Why not?" Horace said. "You're here to work, but there's no reason why you shouldn't sample some of the local scenery while you're here."
"My husband has a naturally suspicious nature," Whitton said.
"You think I had an ulterior motive?" Horace asked Smith.
"It had crossed my mind," Smith admitted.
"Relax. Try some of the baby octopus. Just this morning they were languishing in the sea. Seafood doesn't get much fresher than that."
Smith declined. Horace had given him far too much information for his liking.
The tapas plates were cleared away and Horace ordered another round of drinks. Smith noticed that he was drinking mineral water. He asked him about it.

"I have an important business meeting tomorrow," Horace said. "I need to keep a clear head."

"I thought you'd retired," Smith said.

"Semi-retired. I still have my finger in a number of pies."

He didn't elaborate on this and Smith didn't press further.

"Tell us about Boris Jackson," he said instead. "I'm pretty intrigued how a self-claimed pacifist like yourself happened to befriend a man who was inside for triple murder."

A smile appeared on Horace's face. He took a sip of his water and nodded. "Boris did what he had to do. I told you – sometimes not everything is as it seems."

CHAPTER THIRTY TWO

While Horace Nagel was telling Smith and Whitton the story of Boris Jackson, a white Ford Transit van was on the prowl over a thousand miles away. This was no ordinary hunting expedition – the two predators in the front of the van knew precisely where their prey would be. The success of *The Workshop* depended on hours and hours of careful forward planning. Reconnaissance was essential and the people employed at *The Workshop* were particularly good at it.

The target in this instance was a woman with an unusual pair of eyes. Heterochromia is a condition that affects fewer than one percent of the population, and the type of heterochromia Emily Grant was born with was even rarer. Emily's left eye had been described by some as *sapphire blue*. It was the blue of the waters of the Caribbean, and it formed a distinct contrast to the amber of the right eye. People couldn't help staring at Emily Grant when they first met her, and it was something she'd become accustomed to.

Emily was twenty-nine, and she was married with a daughter. Taylor Grant was eight years old. The two men in the van were aware of this too. They also knew that on Wednesday evenings Emily accompanied Taylor to her ballet class in Holgate. The dance academy was a ten-minute walk from Emily's house in Foxwood and the lesson was an hour long. Every Wednesday Emily would drop Taylor off and walk the hundred metres to a friend's house, where she would have a cup of tea and a chat while she waited for Taylor's class to finish.

Emily had just passed the bakery on Grantham Street when the van drove past. It slowed down just up ahead and stopped twenty metres before Emily's friend's house. The passenger side door opened, and a young man got out. He was staring at a phone, and he looked extremely frustrated. He turned around and smiled at Emily as she approached.

She thought he had a friendly face, and he seemed vaguely familiar. When she got closer, he shrugged his shoulders and showed Emily his phone.

"GPS is playing silly buggers again," he said.

"Are you lost?" Emily asked.

"We've got a delivery to Howe Hill Road, and according to the GPS we've reached our destination."

"This is Grantham Street," Emily said. "Howe Hill Road is further up. Carry on and take the first left onto Howe Hill Court then it's the first right."

"You're a lifesaver," the man said. "Has anyone ever told you, you have the most incredible eyes."

Emily sighed. "Only for my entire life."

"Can I take a photograph?"

This was nothing new to Emily either.

"My name's Luke."

"Emily," she said.

"How about that photo?"

"It's getting dark," Emily said.

"I have a good flash on my phone camera. Sorry to inconvenience you, but could you stand against the side of the van? I reckon the white background will really accentuate the beauty in your eyes."

Emily thought he had a strange way of talking, but he really did have a pleasant face, and she decided he was harmless enough.

She obliged and stood with her back to the side door of the van. The man called Luke took a few photographs in quick succession and checked the phone to see how they'd come out.

"Perfect," he said.

He showed the phone to Emily.

"There's nothing on the screen," she said.

"Why would there be?"

"Do I know you?"

"I don't think so."

"I do," Emily said. "I've seen you before. By the windmill."

Luke smiled at her and gave her a friendly wave, and that's when Emily realised exactly where she'd seen him before.

Luke took the phone from her and tapped the side of the van. Before Emily knew what was happening, the side door slid open, and she felt hands on her arms and face. One of those hands covered her mouth, muffling the scream she was trying to get out. There was a sharp pain in her arm, and she was dragged inside the van. The door closed and as the flow of liquid ice made its way from her arm to her chest, the last thing Emily registered before she drifted off was the scent of a very familiar perfume.

* * *

"Boris Jackson should have been given a medal for what he did."

Horace Nagel picked up some bread and used it to soak up some of the remaining sauce on his plate.

"He was sentenced to life without parole for three murders," Smith said.

"You said sometimes things are not what they seem," Whitton said. "What did you mean by that?"

"Boris was a rare breed," Horace said. "A relic from a bygone era if you like. There are very few noble souls left out there, but he was one of them."

"Who did he kill?" Smith said.

"I'm coming to that," Horace said. "But you need to know a bit of background before I tell you what happened. Boris grew up being bounced around between one foster home to another. His childhood was a wretched one, but he didn't let it define him. He could have been bitter about his circumstances, but he rose above it. He got a good education, and he made up his mind to do something worthwhile with his life. He qualified as a project care worker, and he set about helping other kids in the care system. He knew what it was like, and he thought he could make a difference."

The waiter came to clear the table, and Horace ordered another round of drinks.

"One of the foster homes on Boris's patch was a place in Tadcaster. Big house with eight bedrooms. The people who ran the place passed all the required checks and kids who needed somewhere to go were placed with them. But as I said sometimes not everything is as it seems. Do you know how much a foster child can earn someone who takes them in?"

Smith had no idea. He told Horace as much.

"Up to twenty grand a year," Horace said. "There were eleven kids in that house in Tadcaster. Do the math."

"That is a lot of money," Whitton said.

"Boris sensed that something wasn't right about the Tadcaster place," Horace said. "The children weren't right – there was something *off* about every one of them, and his gut was proven right. He managed to get one of them to talk. It was a fifteen-year-old girl, and what she told him caused him to lose it. It was a catalogue of horrors going back months. Those kids were not only neglected, but they were also abused in the worst possible ways. I won't go into details before we're about to eat, but I'm sure you can imagine what I'm talking about. Like I said, Boris lost it. He saw red and that's all he saw. He followed the three so-called *caregivers* to a restaurant one night and shot all three dead at their table."

"Oh my God," Whitton said.

"He put down the gun," Horace said. "And waited for the police to arrive. He ordered and paid for a beer while he was waiting. He figured he probably wasn't going to get the chance to drink one again."

"That's quite a story," Smith said.

"He deserved a medal," Horace said.

"He killed three people in cold blood. Whatever his motive for doing that was – people cannot go around committing murder."

"Not everything is black and white," Horace said. "There are many shades of grey in between."

The food arrived, and Smith was glad. He wasn't in the mood for a deep, philosophical conversation right now.

"So, now you know why I was drawn to Boris Jackson in prison," Horace said. "I have a talent for knowing what lies beneath the surface. I know how to see inside a person's heart."

"That's quite a talent," Smith said. "This cod dish looks delicious."

"You'll love it," Horace said. "I have the best chef in Valencia."

His phone started to ring. He took it out and looked at the screen.

"Oh dear."

He stood up and walked away from the table without further explanation.

"I wonder what that's all about," Whitton said.

"He's a strange one," Smith said.

Horace returned to the table soon afterwards.

"I apologise for that."

"Bad news?" Smith said.

"I don't really know," Horace said. "That was the captain of *Serenity*. Paddy Carroll died in the master cabin an hour ago."

CHAPTER THIRTY THREE

"It's been confirmed," DI Smyth said. "The woman found by Four Lanes End is Zoe Granger."

Nobody commented on this. Everyone inside the small conference room knew deep down that this was the inevitable outcome.

"Miss Granger had been missing for four days when she was found," DI Smyth said. "Now we have a positive ID we need to try and trace her movements in that time. Where was she in the four days between her disappearing and her ending up dead?"

"Do you think there's a chance that she was taken and kept alive somewhere?" DC King put forward.

"It's possible," DI Smyth said.

"Why?" DC Moore said. "Why keep her alive for all that time if they're planning on killing her and chopping off her head, arms and legs?"

"We don't know, Harry. Right now, we know very little about these people."

"I reckon she was abducted and taken somewhere," Bridge said. "And held prisoner until they decided to kill her."

"We've had another report of a missing woman," DI Smyth said. "Emily Grant took her daughter to a ballet class last night, and she didn't return to pick her up. According to Emily's daughter, her mother usually waits at a friend's house while Emily is at ballet, but the friend confirmed that she didn't turn up yesterday evening."

"Who reported her missing?" DC King said.

"The woman who runs the ballet class tried to contact her," DI Smyth said. "But Emily didn't answer her phone. The daughter had the presence of mind to phone the friend, and it was her who contacted the police."

"What about the husband?" DC Moore said.

"Out of the picture. He and Emily have been divorced for three years. The dance academy is just around the corner from the friend's house and the uniforms that attended retraced the route and carried out a quick door-to-door. A woman who lives a few doors down from the friend remembers seeing a white van parked in the road for a short while. It ties in with the time Emily should have been making her way to her friend's house."

"The camper at the Grantchester campsite told us about a white van too," Bridge remembered. "It could be relevant."

"Unfortunately," DI Smyth said. "The witness couldn't tell us any more than that. It was a white van – that's all."

"What about CCTV?" Bridge said. "Do we know if any of the properties have cameras?"

"It's early days," DI Smyth said. "We'll check out the route Emily usually took from the dance academy to the friend's house, and hopefully we'll get lucky."

"What else do we know about her?" DC King said.

"Very little," DI Smyth said. "She's twenty-nine, divorced and she has an eight-year-old daughter. We'll speak to her family and friends during the course of the day. I spoke to Smith yesterday."

"How is he enjoying his holiday?" Bridge asked.

"It's not a holiday, and he told me something interesting, if slightly disturbing. A friend of Horace Nagel's hinted at something we need to consider. He spoke of megarich clients who are very partial to macabre products."

"Human body parts?" DC Moore said.

"Some of these clients are collectors," DI Smyth said. "And some believe in the healing and restorative properties of healthy human parts. Others are convinced they can achieve immortality by drinking specific human blood."

"That is beyond sick," DC King said.

"It is what it is, Kerry," DI Smyth said. "But it makes sense. Smith also talked about a company we need to take a closer look at. *Artemis Trading*."

"Never heard of them," Bridge said.

"That's irrelevant. The friend of Horace Nagel's seems to think they could be involved in this."

"Where do we even start looking?" Bridge said.

"If they're a listed company," DC Moore said. "We'll be able to find them on the net. And if not, it should be possible to get hold of them via the tax office."

Bridge started to laugh. It was a hearty laugh, and it was rather inappropriate under the circumstances.

"What's got into you?" DI Smyth asked.

"Sorry, sir," Bridge said. "It just strikes me as funny imagining the taxman getting revenue from the sale of human body parts."

"There's something wrong with you," DC Moore said.

"You've been hanging around with Smith for too long," DC King added.

DI Smyth smiled. "Let's move on. Harry, I want you to see what you can find out about this *Artemis Trading*. Bridge, you and Kerry can retrace the route that Emily Grant usually took from the dance studio to her friend's house. Speak to the neighbours again. Someone might remember something they neglected to tell uniform. I'll be carrying out the unenviable task of informing Zoe Granger's parents that their daughter is never coming home."

"When are Smith and Whitton getting back?" Bridge said.

"Smith sent me a message. They've managed to get on an earlier flight. They'll be landing in Leeds Bradford at one, so they should be back on board later this afternoon. We've got a lot to get through today, so I suggest we make a start."

Bridge and DC King got to their feet. DC Moore remained where he was.

"Harry," DI Smyth said.

DC Moore wasn't listening. His eyes were focused on something on the whiteboard at the back. He stood up and walked over to it.

"What's up, Harry?" DI Smyth said.

DC Moore pointed to something on the whiteboard. It was the @ sign.

"Both victims were branded with the @ symbol."

"We know that," Bridge said.

"*Artemis Trading*," DC Moore said. "AT. The @ could stand for AT."

CHAPTER THIRTY FOUR

The shrill notes of Smith's phone alarm caused him to shoot up in the bed. He reached over to find the source of the din and knocked the phone onto the floor in the process. He got out of bed, picked up the offensive device and silenced it. The quiet inside the room didn't last long. The phone on the table next to the wall started to ring. Smith picked it up.
"Hello."
"I have a message for you, sir," a man said.
"Who is this?" Smith asked.
"My name is Peter. I'm phoning from reception. A Horace Nagel left a message asking if you could meet him at the Marina Mar at eight."
"What time is it now?"
"Just after seven."
Smith did some quick calculations in his head. They needed to be at the airport at half-nine, so it would be possible to meet up with Horace Nagel and make it to the airport in time. He thanked the receptionist and replaced the phone handset.

Whitton came out of the bathroom.
"Who were you talking to?"
"Reception," Smith said. "Horace left a message asking to meet him at the marina."
"I wonder what he wants."
He hadn't mentioned anything about seeing them again the night before. They'd said their goodbyes and Smith assumed they probably wouldn't cross paths again.
"I suppose we'll find out when we get there," he said.

Thirty minutes later they were in a taxi heading to the marina. Smith was intrigued and he wondered whether Horace Nagel had some more information for them.

"Don't you think it's strange that he wants to meet at the marina?" Whitton said.

"It's as good a place as any to meet," Smith said.

"His friend died there yesterday," Whitton said. "I just think it's weird that he would want to go there after that."

"I suppose it is a bit odd," Smith agreed.

He paid the taxi driver and asked him if he could stick around. They still needed to get to the airport afterwards. The driver shrugged his shoulders, cranked up the air conditioner and made himself comfortable in his seat. He was asleep in seconds.

"What a life," Smith said.

"Did he say where we're supposed to meet?" Whitton asked. "Horace, I mean."

"The receptionist didn't mention anything."

"We have to check in for the flight in less than two hours," Whitton said. "I hope this isn't going to be a waste of time."

Smith looked around. The marina seemed quieter today. Something occurred to him. If Patrick Carroll had died on his boat, surely there would be a police presence at the marina, but Smith couldn't see any sign of one. He shared his thoughts with Whitton.

"Perhaps the body was taken away last night," she said. "He was riddled with cancer, so his death isn't suspicious."

"I suppose so. Let's go and see if Horace is on the boat."

They made their way to the outer jetties and as they got closer to where *Serenity* was berthed, Smith realised that there was some activity on the yacht. The crew were busy on deck, and it appeared that they were preparing to go out to sea. Smith thought this was odd – why would they be setting sail the morning after the owner of the boat had passed away on board?

Two deckhands were unravelling the mooring lines from the jetty.
"Where are you going?" Smith asked one of them.
"We're heading down to Morocco," the woman replied.
"Morocco? Is it a charter?"
"No, it's just Mr Carroll and Mr Nagel."
"Why is the body being taken to Morocco?" Smith said.
The deckhand looked at him as though he'd grown another head. She hopped back on board and Smith could hear the sound of the engine starting up. There was a surge of water as the bow thrusters did their thing and the yacht slowly drifted away from the jetty.

"Horace!" Smith shouted.
The Dutchman appeared shortly afterwards. He emerged from the cockpit with a ghost. Patrick Carroll was standing next to him, alive and well.
"What the hell is going on?" Smith screamed.
The distance between the boat and the jetty was widening. Soon, Smith knew it would turn and head for the harbour entrance.
"Why did you ask us to meet you here?" Smith said.
"Simply to demonstrate to you that not everything is as it seems," Horace said.
"Why did you tell us that Patrick was dead?" Whitton said.
"Why not?"
"What's going on, Horace?" Smith said.

The Dutchman picked something up from the cockpit and held it up in the air.
"Catch."
Without further warning he threw the package at Smith. It caught Smith off

guard, but he managed to catch it before it ended up in the water behind him. The parcel wasn't heavy. It was a padded A4 envelope and Smith could feel that there was something solid inside.

"What's this?" Smith said.

"A parting gift," Horace said.

Smith tore the envelope open. Inside was a single sheet of paper and something metallic. He opened the paper and read the address that had been written on it. It was an address he recognised – it was somewhere in York.

"You won't find me," Horace said. "Don't bother looking for me."

The noise from the engine was louder and Smith knew there wasn't much time left.

"What's the address on the paper?" he said.

"It's where you'll find *The Workshop*. Don't worry – I'm ceasing operations as from now. I'm getting too old for this nonsense. Have a safe flight home."

"Wait," Smith shouted. "What exactly are you telling me?"

He reached inside the envelope and took out the metallic object. It was disc-shaped, and it was roughly the size of a beermat.

"Tell Jeremy I send my regards," Horace said.

The yacht was almost clear of the marina now.

"I thought he might want a memento from his beloved car. Adios."

Smith looked at the disc in his hand. It was the steering wheel logo from a Range Rover.

CHAPTER THIRTY FIVE

"We were well and truly fooled."
Smith was exhausted. He and Whitton had driven straight to the station from Leeds Bradford airport, and now they were explaining to DI Smyth what had happened at the marina.

"Horace Nagel took us for a ride," Whitton said.

After watching the stern of *Serenity* getting further and further out to sea Smith and Whitton had raced to the taxi, woken the driver and told him to step on it to the airport. Once there, Smith had logged onto the Wi-Fi and forwarded the address Horace Nagel had written down to DI Smyth. He'd mobilized the troops, and they were there within the hour. Once again, Horace Nagel's words would come back to haunt Smith.

Not everything is as it seems.

If Smith was hoping to find any evidence of the activities of *The Workshop* he was going to be sorely disappointed. The location Horace had given them was a disused warehouse on the outskirts of the city and it had been abandoned. The carcasses of sixteen vehicles were lined up inside the building. All of them had been stripped for parts. This was indeed once a workshop, but it wasn't the workshop Smith had hoped for.

The steering wheel badge from Superintendent Smyth's Range Rover was on his nephew's desk. Smith glanced at it.

"Nagel was the brains behind the carjacking all along," he said. "Fuck it – I really thought he could help us with *The Workshop*, but he was playing us the whole time."

"He's probably going to get away with it," DI Smyth said. "We have absolutely no jurisdiction in the waters of the Mediterranean. And it'll be even more difficult if he does dock in Morocco."

"What about Interpol?" Whitton said.

"Without reasonable grounds, we cannot justify an Interpol investigation. All we have on Nagel is a veiled confession and a steering wheel badge that, in theory could have come from any Range Rover."

"He has to show his face in York sooner or later," Whitton said. "He has a house here."

"He doesn't," DI Smyth said. "Not really. The place in Fulford is leased. A years' rent was paid in advance by a company that no longer exists. The lease is due to run out next month."

"And I bet if we were to check," Smith said. "We'll find that the same goes for the apartment in Valencia. He strung me along and I fell for it hook, line, and sinker."

"Let it be a lesson to you," DI Smyth said. "And move past it. What's done is done, and he did say he was ceasing operations in the carjacking thing, so that's something at least."

"I'm such a bloody fool," Smith said. "I really thought he was legitimate."

"Get over it," DI Smyth said. "We have more pressing matters to attend to."

Smith's gaze found the Range Rover badge again.

"Are you going to give that to Uncle Jeremy?"

"Get out," DI Smyth said. "Both of you. You have a lot of catching up to do."

Smith left the office and headed up to the canteen. It had been a long, draining day and he needed some strong coffee. Bridge and DC Moore were sitting at the table by the window. Smith walked over to the coffee machine and Bridge started to slow clap behind him. DC Moore followed suit.

Smith took his coffee to the table. Bridge and DC Moore were still busy with their patronising applause.

"Fuck off," Smith said. "I was an idiot – I admit it. Nagel blindsided me good and proper."

The handclaps stopped.

"The chop-shop is going to be a logistical nightmare," Bridge said. "There were over a dozen chopped up vehicles in that warehouse."

"It's not our nightmare," Smith said. "It's someone else's problem. What a day."

He took a drink of coffee.

"I spent all morning taking a close look at Artemis Trading," DC Moore said. "Based on your Dutch friend's tip-off. Thanks a lot for that, Sarge."

"It was actually his Irish friend who mentioned them."

DC Moore rolled his eyes.

"What did you find out?" Smith asked.

"They're a listed export business."

"Where are they based?"

"Here in York."

"They still could be worth checking out," Smith said.

"They're a legit company who specialise in exporting luxury vehicles – mostly to China and the Far East."

"Interesting," Smith said.

"It's not interesting at all," DC Moore said. "All of their export licenses are in place, and as far as I could see from the info on the Internet, the company is as genuine as they come."

"That means nothing," Smith said.

"Horace Nagel pulled the wool over your eyes about the chop-shop," Bridge pointed out. "Why would you take his cohort seriously about the info on Artemis Trading?"

"I don't know," Smith said. "The Irishman seemed to know a hell of a lot about *The Workshop*. He mentioned things that seemed entirely plausible, considering what we've seen done to the victims."

"Forget about it," Bridge said.

Smith rubbed his eyes and drank some more coffee.

"No," he said. "The first victim had her head chopped off."

"Zoe Granger," Bridge said. "We've got an ID for her."

"Zoe Granger," Smith repeated. "Had her head chopped off and Patrick Carroll just happened to mention something about billionaires who collect trophies like that. The second victim was an athlete. This also ties in with what Patrick said. And we just happen to have a missing woman with a very rare blood type. That Irishman knew far too much."

"Have you considered that he might know this because he's involved?" Bridge said.

Smith looked him in the eye.

"It's worth thinking about," Bridge said. "What do you actually know about the bloke?"

"He's knocking on heaven's door," Smith said. "And he's extremely wealthy."

"Knocking on heaven's door?" DC Moore said.

"It's a song," Smith explained. "Patrick Carroll has lung cancer, and he hasn't got long left."

"He was probably lying about that too," Bridge said. "I think you're losing your touch. You never used to be so gullible."

Smith nodded and stood up.

"I need a smoke."

"You need a lot more than that, mate," Bridge said.

CHAPTER THIRTY SIX

As Smith was on his way out, PC Griffin and PC Hill were coming in.

"I need to talk to you, Sarge," PC Griffin said. "About the accident involving your car yesterday."

Smith really didn't feel like an altercation with the piggy-eyed PC right now.

"I was in Spain yesterday," he said.

"I'm aware of that, but it doesn't alter the fact that the kid was driving your car. We need to file a report."

"The *kid* had my permission to drive that car, Griffin," Smith said. "I reckon if he's old enough to drive, he's old enough to face the consequences of his actions on his own, don't you?"

PC Griffin didn't reply to this. His mouth opened wide, and his beady eyes shifted from side to side.

"I'm glad we've got that cleared up," Smith said. "I'm sure you have work to do."

He walked around the side of the station without waiting for confirmation of that.

Once again, DCI Chalmers was outside too. He was smoking a cigarette next to the wall.

"Boss," Smith said in greeting.

He lit his own cigarette.

"You look like shit," Chalmers said.

"I look exactly how I feel."

"Fair enough. I heard about Nagel making a tit out of you."

"Thanks for that," Smith said. "I can't figure out why he did it."

"He's a sneaky bastard, that's why."

"I really had no idea he was behind the carjacking gang. He played me like a pro. He even made out that his friend had died the evening after we'd spent an afternoon on his superyacht. That part really confused me."

"What's the name of the friend?"

"Patrick Carroll," Smith said.

"Shifty Irishman?"

"I thought he was alright."

"Does he still look like he's at death's door?"

"He has lung cancer," Smith said. "He really does look like he doesn't have long left."

"Patrick Carroll looked like that thirty years ago. He was lying to you."

Smith's cigarette had gone out. He lit it again and took a long drag. He wondered if anything Horace Nagel and Patrick Carroll had told them had any ounce of truth in it.

"What's the progress with the *Workshop* thing?" Chalmers asked.

"We've got an ID for the first victim," Smith said. "Zoe Granger. She was a beautiful young woman in the prime of her life, and some wealthy sick fuck had enough money to buy her. She was killed to order, and she was chopped up to fulfil the terms of that order."

"What are you going to do about Nagel?" Chalmers said.

"The boss reckons he's home free. One of the deckhands on Patrick Carroll's yacht told me they were heading for Morocco and we have no jurisdiction in that part of the world. All we have tying Nagel to the carjackers so far is an ambiguous confession and the badge from the Super's Range Rover."

Chalmers laughed. "I would love to be a fly on the wall when he hears about that."

"I don't think the DI is going to tell him. We've got the location of the chop-shop and there'll be a full investigation, but I'll bet a years' salary that there will be nothing there that can be linked to Nagel. He will have covered his tracks and for all we know he's halfway to South America by now. The carjacking thing isn't important anymore. It's over, and all the vehicles that were stolen were insured anyway. I'm not going to waste any time on it."

"Do you have any leads whatsoever in the *Workshop* investigation?" Chalmers said.

"Not a sausage. Patrick Carroll gave us the name of a company we should look into, but that will probably be a wild goose chase. We're still no closer to figuring out where these bastards are operating out of, and I'm running out of ideas. We've got two bodies and a missing woman, and I don't think this is the end of it. As long as there are superrich depraved individuals out there, the people involved in this are going to stay open for business."

Chalmers stubbed out his cigarette. "Go back to the beginning."
Smith couldn't help rolling his eyes. "See if something jumps out at us – something we missed the first time?"

"It's proven to be effective in the past."

"With respect, boss," Smith said. "I don't think traditional detection methods are going to work this time. This one is so different to anything we've ever come across that we need to think differently. The motive is outrageous to the point of being beyond belief. What kind of people are they? Who would even dream up a business like this? And how do they advertise their services?"

"Focus on what you know," Chalmers said. "Before you start speculating about questions you can't yet answer."

"What do we know?" Smith asked himself. "Two young people are dead, and another woman is missing."

"How are they doing it?"

"We know very little about the first two victims," Smith said. "But it looks like the first missing woman was taken when she was on her way home after donating blood."

"What does that tell you?"

"It's clear that they've done a lot of homework beforehand," Smith said. "They knew exactly where Kirsty Davies would be. She was taken because of her rare blood type. Fuck – how did they know she was AB negative?"
"Now you're starting to sound like the Smith I remember working with," Chalmers said. "I was worried you were losing your touch for a bit there."

"Kirsty is still alive," Smith said. "I'm certain she's still alive. She's much more valuable to them if she can provide them with a constant supply of blood. They're holding her prisoner somewhere in the city and it makes me sick to the stomach because I have no idea where to start looking."
"Start acting like a detective then," Chalmers said. "Instead of whining like a spoilt teenager. Use that twisted brain of yours how it's supposed to be used, and you might just get somewhere. I'd better get back. Do you want me to tell the Super that we've recovered some of his precious car?"
"Go for it. He can have the badge framed and hung in his office. Thanks for the pep talk."
"I'll have no more of this namby pamby bollocks," Chalmers said. "You're an honorary Yorkshireman now – grow a pair of balls and start acting like one."

CHAPTER THIRTY SEVEN

"Emily Grant has a very rare condition," DI Smyth began the afternoon briefing. "She has something called heterochromia which means her eyes are different colours. In Mrs Grant's case the effect is especially striking. Harry."

DC Moore tapped the keypad of the laptop and soon afterwards a photograph appeared on the screen at the back of the room.

"That's amazing," Bridge commented.

Emily Grant really was an extraordinary looking woman. Her delicate features aside, it was her eyes that everyone inside the room were drawn to now. The photograph was a close-up of her face and it looked like it had been taken by a professional photographer in a studio.

Her left eye was azure blue. The close-up enabled the team to see specks of green in the iris. The makeup Emily was wearing was subtle, but it accentuated the remarkable colour of the eye. Her right eye wasn't so striking but it was unusual, nevertheless. The amber had a copper hue to it, and the iris was rimmed with a much darker brown, highlighting the golden brown within. It was a truly unique combination, and Smith had never seen eyes like them.

"She was taken for her eyes, wasn't she?" he put forward.

DI Smyth looked at the photograph. "I believe she was. We know that she dropped her daughter off at the dance academy yesterday evening at seven and she then walked to a friend's house a short distance away. She does this every Wednesday which leads me to believe these people are aware of her movements. They knew exactly where she would be, and they knew when to strike."

"A witness remembered seeing a white van parked on the road where the friend lives," Bridge said. "We spoke to her again, but she couldn't be any more precise than that. It was a white Ford Transit, and I think that's what they used to transport her after they abducted her. We drew a blank with any CCTV cameras in the area, and none of the other neighbours recalled seeing anything out of the ordinary yesterday evening."

"Do we think they've been watching her for a while?" DC King said.

"They were aware of her Wednesday routine," Smith said. "And that's what we need to focus our efforts on. Kirsty Davies was taken shortly after she gave blood. They were aware of the blood drive, and they were also aware of her rare blood type. How did they know this?"

"We need to find out who is in charge of organising the blood drives," DI Smyth said. "And we need to find out more about Emily Grant."

"It's important that we speak to the daughter," Smith said.

"She's eight years old," DC Moore said.

"What's your point, Harry?" Smith said.

"I don't think she'll be able to tell us anything useful."

"You'd be surprised," Whitton said. "I agree – if someone has been watching Emily Grant for a while it's possible the daughter might have seen something suspicious."

"Are we working on the assumption that Mrs Grant is dead?" DC Moore said.

"Until we have a body," Smith said. "We assume that she's still alive, and if that's the case we haven't got time to waste on dumb questions like the one you just asked."

"I was just thinking out loud."

"I'd prefer it if you didn't," Smith said. "Unless you have something productive to bring up."

"Right," DI Smyth said. "Smith, you and Whitton can talk to the little girl. Taylor is her name and I'm sure the rest of you will agree that you two have the most experience where girls Taylor's age are concerned."

Smith nodded. "Girls that age are an alien species. Where is she now?"
"With the grandparents," DI Smyth said. "I don't need to remind you that you need to tread carefully with Taylor *and* the grandparents. We don't want to give them cause for alarm when we don't know the exact details of Emily's disappearance."
"Perhaps it would be better to speak to Taylor on her own."
"Is that allowed?" DC Moore said.
"It is," Smith confirmed. "It's not a formal interview, and as Taylor isn't in police custody we're well within our rights to have a chat to her without an adult being present. Whether the grandparents will agree to it is a different kettle of fish altogether. We can't force them to let us get on with it, but we can persuade them that it's in Emily's best interests to do so."
"Could you get moving on that then?" DI Smyth said. "You can get the details of the grandparents from the front desk."

"Are we going to take a closer look at Artemis Trading?" DC Moore asked. "Because as far as I could see they operate a legitimate business. Their prime export is high-end vehicles, and I can't see them being involved in the *Workshop*."
"We can't rule them out completely," DI Smyth said.
"The tip-off came from a known criminal, sir," DC Moore said. "It's hardly reliable."
"You'd be surprised how many cases have been cracked because of those kinds of tip-offs, Harry."
"Go and check them out," Smith said. "Even if it's just to tick them off the list."

He got up from his seat. Whitton did the same. Smith cast a glance at the photograph at the back of the room. His eyes found Emily Grant's and he made a silent promise to himself to do everything he could to bring her back home to her daughter.

* * *

Emily Grant's first thought when she regained consciousness was that there was a familiar smell somewhere close by. It was the scent of a perfume she knew well. It was a floral blend of jasmine, rose and sweet lily and Emily had grown up with that scent in her life. The perfume was Anais Anais and her mother Hilda had worn nothing else.

But why could she smell it now? It was on her clothes and in her hair, and she had no idea why this was. Emily's next thought was of her daughter. Where was Taylor?

"Taylor," she called out.

Nothing. She tried again with the same result. She open her eyes, blinked a few times, and that's when she realised there was something tied around her head, covering both eyes. She raised an arm to remove the offensive blindfold but she couldn't move it. Both her wrists were bound to the arms of the chair she was sitting on.

"Hello," she shouted. "Where am I?'

"You need to keep quiet."

The voice was no louder than a whisper and it was a woman's voice.

"Who are you?" Emily said.

"Shh. They can hear us."

"What am I doing here?" Emily whispered.

"What do you remember?"

"I remember a van and a man who wanted to take my photograph and then I woke up here."

"They took you like they took me."

"Who took me?" Emily asked.

"I don't know. All I know is one of them is called Luke."

"I need to go. I need to go to my daughter."

"They're keeping us prisoner here."

"We need to find a way to get out," Emily said. "I need to see my daughter."

"I'm too weak."

"What's your name?"

"Kirsty."

"I'm Emily, and I have to get out of here. You need to help me."

"I'm too weak."

"What did they do to you?"

"They took too much of my blood."

Emily Grant didn't know what was happening, but she did know it was very bad. She filled her lungs with air and let rip with a scream, the likes of which she'd never screamed before.

CHAPTER THIRTY EIGHT

Taylor Grant was a pretty, slender child with long red hair. Smith noticed that she too had different coloured eyes, and he wondered whether Emily's rare condition was hereditary.

Emily's father Colin had answered the door and after Smith had explained the nature of their visit, he'd invited them in without any questions. He led them to the living room and asked them to take a seat. Taylor had excused herself and gone upstairs to her room shortly after Smith and Whitton arrived. The house was in need of some serious maintenance. The wallpaper on the walls was peeling off in places, and the tatty fake leather lounge suite looked like it was procured from a skip. Smith deduced that Emily's parents didn't have an awful lot of money. Colin took a seat in a single armchair and remained silent.

Emily's mother, Hilda had a lot more to say.
"What are you doing about finding my daughter?"
"We're doing everything we can," Whitton said. "We've got every available officer out looking for her – we're busy with a thorough door-to-door, and we'll be speaking to everyone who knows her."
"That's what we're doing here actually," Smith said. "We really need to speak to Taylor."
"She's eight years' old," Hilda said. "I don't know what you expect her to tell you."
"We suspect that Emily's disappearance may have something to do with an ongoing case of ours," Whitton said.
"What ongoing case? What's going on? Is there something I need to be aware of?"
"I'm afraid we can't go into the details," Smith said.

"I'm not buying that," Hilda said. "This is my daughter we're talking about. If you know something about her going missing, I have a right to know."

"We understand your concerns, Mrs Grant," Whitton said.

"Lewis," Hilda corrected. "It's Hilda Lewis. You can't even get that right."

"Let them speak, love," Colin said.

"Who asked you?" Hilda said. "Our daughter is missing, and you don't seem to care."

"Of course I care," Colin said. "The police are doing everything they can."

"She's still missing, isn't she?"

"I'll put the kettle on to make some coffee," Colin said.

He left the room without asking if anyone wanted anything to drink.

"Well?" Hilda said. "Are you going to find my daughter or not?"

"Like my colleague said," Smith said. "We're doing everything we can. It's early days, but we're hoping to make some progress soon."

Hilda snorted, and Smith caught a whiff of something sweet. It was a perfume he'd come across before.

"Progress?" Hilda said. "I'll believe that when I see my daughter again."

"We really need to speak to Taylor," Smith said. "Preferably without you and Mrs Lewis present."

"You're not allowed to do that."

"Actually, we are," Whitton said. "She's under no obligation to talk to us, but we believe she can help us to get her mother back."

"Do I need to call my lawyer?" Hilda asked.

"You're well within your rights to do that," Smith said. "But I don't think it would serve any purpose other than to delay things further. In a missing persons' case time is of the essence, and we need to move quickly."

"If you could go and get Taylor for us," Whitton said. "We'll ask her a few questions and we'll leave you in peace."

"I don't want her traumatised any more than she already is," Hilda said.

"She has no idea what's happened to her mother."

"We won't upset her," Smith said.

"We have experience in this kind of thing," Whitton added. "It won't take long."

Hilda seemed to be considering this. She focused her gaze on a photograph on the mantelpiece. Smith realised that it was the same photo that had been on display in the small conference room earlier. Hilda snorted again.

"I'll go and see if she wants to talk to you. If she wants me or Colin to sit with her when you speak to her, you'll have to accept that. Or do I have to make that call to my lawyer to get her to explain it to you?"

"I don't think that will be necessary," Smith said.

"If you could just go and get her," Whitton said.

Hilda left the room and Smith looked at the photo on the mantelpiece. Colin still hadn't returned with the coffee.

"She's a bit overbearing, isn't she?" Whitton said.

"Just a bit," Smith said. "Her daughter is missing and she's doing everything she can to get in our way. There's something not right about her."

"She could be in shock. It affects people in different ways."

"No," Smith said. "Something else is going on with Hilda Lewis."

"She was right about that though."

"About what?"

"The surname thing," Whitton said. "The name I got from Baldwin was Hilda Grant. Emily still uses her married name even though she's been divorced for a few years. Perhaps Hilda thinks if we can't get a simple thing like that right, what chance do we have of bringing her daughter home?"

Hilda, Colin and Taylor came into the room together. There was still no sign of the coffee Colin had offered.

"She'll speak to you," Hilda said. "But if you do anything to upset her, I'll have my lawyer onto you quicker than you can say *Hilda Grant.*"
For some reason this made Smith smile.
"We won't do anything to upset her," he said. "If you could leave us now, we'd appreciate it."

"Taylor," Whitton said when her grandparents had gone. "You're a ballet dancer, aren't you?"
Taylor was sitting on the single armchair. She was sitting up straight with her hands on her knees. It was obvious she did ballet from her posture. She nodded. "I've been dancing for four years."
"Wow," Whitton said.
"You know why we're here, don't you?" Smith said.
Another nod.
"That's good. We're not going to treat you like a kid because you're eight. We have two eight-year-old girls at home, and if there's one thing I've learned it's that they're a lot smarter than people think."
This resulted in a smile from Taylor. The smile reached her eyes and Smith found himself staring at them. They weren't as striking as her mother's – Taylor's were two different shades of blue, but they were still extremely unusual.

"Your mum takes you to ballet class every Wednesday, doesn't she?" Whitton said.
Taylor nodded.
"You dance at the academy in Holgate," Smith said. "Have you always danced there?"
"Only since March this year."
"Where did you go before?" Whitton said.
"A studio in Foxwood."
"Why did you move?" Smith said.

"Holgate is closer," Taylor said. "But we couldn't afford it before."

"It always comes down to money, doesn't it?" Smith said. "I really don't like money."

Taylor didn't comment on this.

"Mum got a new job," she said. "So, it meant I could go to Holgate."

"How many other dancers are there?" Whitton said.

"Sixteen," Taylor said.

"What about the teachers?" Smith said. "How many teachers are there?"

"They're called instructors."

"There you go," Smith said. "I didn't know that – you're smarter than me. How many instructors are there at the academy?"

"On Wednesdays there are three."

Smith made a mental note to get their details.

"Do you always walk to the academy?" he said.

"Mum doesn't have a car," Taylor said. "And it's not far."

"Your mum waits at a friend's house while you're in class, doesn't she?" Whitton said.

"Katie. She lives round the corner from the academy."

"Has your mum always done that?" Smith said.

"Yes."

"Do many people know about your class on Wednesday?" Whitton said.

"A few."

"I suppose you talk to your friends about it," Smith said.

"Sometimes."

"Who else knows?"

"Nanna and Granddad," Taylor said.

"Anybody else?" Smith asked.

"I don't think so."

"Taylor," Whitton said. "We need you to think hard before you answer the next question. Can you remember anything strange about any of the times you've walked to ballet class in the past few weeks?"

"Strange?" Taylor said.

"Anything suspicious," Smith said. "You know what suspicious means, don't you?"

Taylor nodded.

"It might have been someone who looked like they were watching you," Smith said. "Or perhaps you felt like you were being followed. Can you remember anything like that?"

"I don't think so. Are you going to find my mum?"

"We are?" Smith said.

Whitton's subtle side glance told him he shouldn't have said that. Smith remembered his silent promise back at the station and he was now even more determined to keep it.

"Maybe you can remember somebody in particular," he said. "Somebody who always seemed to be there when you walked to ballet class."

"I can't remember," Taylor said.

"It's alright," Whitton said.

"Can I go now?"

"We're almost finished," Smith told her.

"I have to practice."

"We're nearly done. Are there usually many people around when you walk to ballet class?"

"Not really," Taylor said.

"But there are people on the streets?"

Taylor nodded.

"Do you or your mum ever talk to any of these people?" Whitton said.

"Mum says hello to people she knows."

"Do you say hello too?" Smith said.

"No."

"Can you think really hard?" Smith said. "Can you remember seeing the same person at roughly the same time during your walk?"

Taylor's eyes shifted to the wall opposite her. Smith waited for her to speak.

"There's a man."

"Do you know him?" Smith said.

"No," Taylor said. "He's there sometimes when we walk to the academy."

"Where exactly do you see him?" Whitton said.

"He walks on the other side of the road, by the windmill."

"And you've seen him more than once?" Smith said.

"He's usually there when we walk past the windmill," Taylor said.

"Can you describe him?" Whitton said.

"He looks nice."

"What do you mean by that?" Smith said.

"He has a nice face," Taylor said.

"Has your mum ever spoken to him?"

"No. He's always on the other side of the road. But he sometimes waves."

"He waves at you?"

Another nod. "And mum waves back. I think she likes him."

CHAPTER THIRTY NINE

The man sitting behind the reception desk at the offices of Artemis Trading didn't even bother to hide his irritation when Bridge showed him his ID and informed him of the reason he and DC Moore were there. He sighed loudly and shook his head. The name on his badge was Frank Darwin.

"We're about to close."

"That's unfortunate," Bridge said. "We'd like to speak to someone who can give us some information about the business."

"What for?"

"You don't need to know that," DC Moore said.

"Do you have a warrant?"

"We don't need one," Bridge said. "Can you help us or not?"

After letting out another sigh, Frank stood up and walked down the corridor next to the desk.

He returned shortly afterwards with a man in an expensive looking suit.

"Can I help you gentlemen?"

"I hope so," Bridge said.

He introduced himself and DC Moore.

"You're not here about my outstanding parking tickets, are you?"

"No," Bridge said. "We'd like to have a word about the nature of the business. Would that be possible?"

"I don't see why not. Follow me."

He led them to a spacious office and told them to take a seat. He introduced himself as Donald Cooper as they walked.

"What do you want to know?"

He made himself comfortable behind the desk.

"What is it you do here?" DC Moore said. "Your position in the company, I mean."

"CFO," Donald said. "Basically, I oversee the financial side of the operations. Why are two detectives so interested in an export business? Surely, if anything is amiss it falls under the remit of customs and excise."

"Artemis Trading has come up in an ongoing investigation," Bridge said. "This is just a routine enquiry. Can you tell us a bit about the business?"

"There isn't much to tell," Donald said. "We source high-end vehicles for wealthy clients all around the world – they pay for the goods, and we ship them out."

"Where are the cars stored before they're exported?" DC Moore said. "I assume they leave by boat."

"Of course," Donald said. "You do not put a fleet of cars on an aeroplane."

"York is miles from the sea," Bridge said. "It's a strange place to run an export business out of."

"Here at the offices we merely deal with the logistics. The vehicles themselves are sorted at a warehouse in Grimsby. From there, they're loaded into containers and shipped to their final destinations."

"Does Artemis Trading own the warehouse and the containers?" DC Moore said. "Or do you use the services of a separate shipping company?"

"The warehouse is owned by a subsidiary company of ours," Donald said. "But we subcontract the shipping to a specialised operation. It doesn't pay to keep all one's eggs in one basket, does it?"

Bridge had no idea what he was talking about.

"Let me see if I've understood this," he said. "The offices in York are where the orders are processed, and where the payments are received."

"That's correct," Donald said.

"But the cars are stored and shipped from a warehouse in Grimsby."

"Also correct."

"Why Grimsby?"

"Why not? It's the busiest port in the northeast."

"How long are the cars kept in the warehouse?" DC Moore said.

"That depends on a number of factors," Donald said.

"What factors?"

"Why are you so interested in Artemis Trading?"

"Could you please just answer the question." Bridge said.

"The vehicles are stored until such time that it makes financial sense to prepare them for export. It's essential to fill a container to the brim. I'm sure you'll appreciate that."

"How much time are we talking about?" DC Moore said. "On average."

"Sometimes as long as two to three months," Donald said. "Usually less. As the warehouse itself is in essence owned by Artemis Trading it doesn't cost the company any extra to have to take up warehouse space."

"I assume the cars are kept secure," DC Moore said.

"Of course," Donald said. "The warehouse has state of the art security in place, and we employ security officers around the clock."

"Who has access to the cars?" Bridge said.

"Only people who are authorised to be at the warehouse are allowed in."

"You didn't answer the question. Would it be possible to get a list of those people?"

"You do realise that I am not obliged to give out that kind of information without a legal document ordering me to."

"I do," Bridge confirmed. "But that sort of thing takes time, and we've got a lot on at the moment. I'm asking you to help us out a bit."

"As CFO you'll have access to the personnel records," DC Moore said. "You'd really be doing us a favour. Between you and me, I don't think Artemis Trading has any connection to our investigation and we're really here to tick you off a list."

"A routine enquiry?"

"Exactly," Bridge said. "You can email the list to the address on there." He handed Donald one of his cards.

"And perhaps you could also give us a list of the board of directors," he added.

"You can get that from our website," Donald said. "Artemis Trading is a listed company and as such, the list of the members of the board is public knowledge."

"But any information about the warehouse isn't," DC Moore said. "You're not obliged to provide the details of any subsidiary companies."

"Correct." Donald turned his attention to his laptop.

After a minute or so he looked at Bridge. "All done. Will there be anything else?"

"Where did the name come from?" Bridge asked. "Artemis Trading – it's an unusual name."

"Artemis was a Greek goddess. She was the daughter of Zeus and the twin sister of Apollo. She was the goddess of the hunt, among other things."

"Interesting," Bridge said.

"She was also the goddess of childbirth, care of children and chastity."

"And someone named a car export business after her?" DC Moore said. "Don't you think that's a bit weird?"

"It's not my place to have an opinion on the matter," Donald said. "Are we done here?"

"I think so," Bridge said.

CHAPTER FORTY

"We've got two more bodies."

DI Smyth didn't bother with any pleasantries.

Smith looked at his phone as if it was suddenly giving off a foul smell.

"Say that again," he dared.

"Two dead bodies," DI Smyth said. "A man and a teenage girl. They were found together in one of the allotments in Holgate. Either these people are getting lazy, or they were dumped together for a reason."

"Do we know if this is connected to *The Workshop*?"

"Without a shadow of a doubt. The girl has had her hands and feet amputated and the man has no chest left. It's the same people."

"We're not expected to attend, are we?" Smith said.

"I don't think that's necessary."

"Thank fuck for that. Whitton and me are both knackered and I've got a bollocking to hand out to a teenage boy. What do we know about the victims?"

"Nothing. Neither of them had any ID on them, and I'm afraid it's another case of waiting for someone to miss them. What did you get from the young girl?"

"She mentioned a man who was there a few times when she and Emily walked to the ballet class. She said he would smile at her mum and wave at her. She also told us that her mum waved back. I think Emily knows him."

"Did she give you a description?"

"Nothing that will help us. Average height and build with what she described as a friendly face. What did you and Kerry get from the university?"

"The blood drives are very popular," DI Smyth said. "On average they have between forty and fifty people donating blood at the drives, and it's not only students who can go there to give blood. We got a list of the donors, but I think it's a very long shot. Bridge and Harry didn't have much to report from the visit to Artemis Trading either. I'd better go – Webber is trying to get my attention."

* * *

DI Smyth walked over to the inner cordon and put his phone back inside his pocket. Grant Webber lifted up the tape and DI Smyth ducked underneath.

"What have you found?" he asked.

"Both of them have been branded," Webber said. "Identical brands to the others – the @ sign, but that's not what I want to show you. You might want to take a few deep breaths."

DI Smyth did so. He closed his eyes and breathed in deeply. He held the air in his lungs for as long as possible and breathed out slowly through his nose. He opened his eyes and dared to look downwards. The bodies had been covered with plastic sheets, and Webber was crouching down, ready to uncover one of them.

The first thing that occurred to DI Smyth was the girl didn't look like she was dead. Her eyes were open and her expression was somewhat peaceful. She appeared to have fallen asleep without remembering to close her eyes. DI Smyth didn't think she was much older than sixteen. Her arms were crossed over her chest and it was clear that she had been placed in this position. Both of her hands had been removed. Her feet had also been amputated, and DI Smyth's eyes were drawn to the stumps.

"No sign of other injuries," he commented.

"No," Webber confirmed. "I think she was left to bleed out."

"Poor girl," DI Smyth said. "What is it you wanted to show me?"

"A clue to her identity," Webber said. "She's wearing a school uniform."

DI Smyth couldn't understand what he meant. The girl was dressed in a white shirt and a dark grey skirt.

"How do you know that?" he asked.

"The skirt she's wearing is unique. See the subtle stripe on the waistband and the hem."

DI Smyth could see it. It was darker in colour."

"Billie recognised it," Webber said. "She thinks it's one of the skirts the girls wear at Heworth High. It's an all-girls school and Billie's sister attended it a few years ago."

"Is she absolutely sure?" DI Smyth said.

"Positive. The skirt has to be ordered from a specialist outlet. It's not something you'd find in any high street clothing shop."

DI Smyth looked carefully at the skirt. He didn't know much about clothing, but he could see that the quality was exceptional.

"Why hasn't anybody missed her? We've had no reports of a schoolgirl going missing."

"It's a mystery," Webber said.

"Why do you think they only amputated her hands and feet?"

"I imagine the answer to that will become clear when you're able to identify her."

"What did they do to the man?" DI Smyth said.

"It was an exact replica of the bloke found by the railway tracks," Webber said. "Looks like his internal organs were taken. And if I'm not mistaken, this bloke is also a sportsman. His muscle definition suggests he's a serious athlete. Unfortunately, we found nothing on his person to help with an ID."

"Another case of wait for someone to report him missing?"

"I'm afraid so. I don't like this, Oliver."

"You're not the only one. These people are ruthless, and they're more organised than we initially believed. How the hell do they snatch people without arousing suspicion?"

"You've answered that already," Webber said. "We're dealing with an exceptional team of criminals, and I'm starting to think that we're out of our depth."

"I've never heard you say that before."

"I've never seen anything like this before," Webber said.

CHAPTER FORTY ONE

"Do you want to tell me what the hell you were thinking?"
Smith was sitting opposite Darren Lewis in the kitchen. He'd summoned the teenager as soon as he and Whitton got home. He was already making headway with his second beer.

"It was an accident," Darren explained. "It could have happened to anyone."
"It happened to you," Smith said. "In my car, and why did it have to be a police car you slammed into the back of."
"There was hardly any damage. You can't even tell the Sierra was in an accident."
"Tell me exactly what happened," Smith said.
He finished his beer and opened another one.

"I was parked behind the police car," Darren said. "I had to park pretty close because there wasn't much space on the road. It's always difficult to find parking outside my parents' house. I left the car in gear like I always do"
"I don't," Smith said. "The car has something called a handbrake."
"My dad always taught us that you shouldn't overuse the handbrake," Darren said. "It puts strain on the cable."
"I'm not interested in a lesson in car maintenance."
"That's what happened," Darren said. "I started the engine without taking it out of gear. It shot forward and stalled. It was a minor ding. My dad offered to fix the police car but that PC Griffin wasn't having any of it. He wanted to arrest me for damaging police property."
"That's not going to happen," Smith said.
"Griffin thought I'd done it on purpose. I didn't – I'm not that stupid."
"I know you're not."

"Lucy said you're not insured," Darren said.

"It slipped my mind," Smith said. "Technically you were driving without insurance."

"Am I going to get points on my license?"

"Not if I can help it. I'll figure something out."

"The police shouldn't have even been there," Darren said. "My dad hasn't been in trouble for years."

"That's just how it is," Smith told him. "It's how we operate."

"Can I go?" Darren asked. "I have some IT work I need to get finished before the weekend."

"Go on then," Smith said.

Darren stood up.

"Oh, and Darren," Smith said.

"Yes?"

"Thanks for taking care of the girls."

"No problem," Darren said. "I'm really sorry about the accident. It wasn't my fault."

"I know it wasn't. Get out of here."

Darren lingered for a moment and for a split-second Smith sensed he was going to give him a hug.

"I'm going out for a smoke," he said before Darren got the chance.

Outside, the air was crisp and there wasn't a breath of wind. The heat of Valencia was now just a distant memory, and it was one that Smith would be happy to erase from his mind. It had been a humiliating trip and Smith didn't care to dwell on it. He lit a cigarette and closed his eyes. He wondered how many more people would be taken for their body parts. He knew instinctively that this was far from over. As long as there were depraved individuals out there with a bank balance that enabled them to fulfil their sick fantasies, there would be a market for anything.

He recapped what they knew so far about *The Workshop* and it didn't take long. Four bodies had been found, and two women were still missing. He wondered if he would be able to keep his promise to Taylor Grant. The eight-year-old girl couldn't understand where her mum had gone, and it was breaking Smith's heart. He felt utterly powerless, and he didn't like it one little bit. He really didn't know if he was going to be able to reunite Taylor with her mother.

* * *

Emily Grant was woken mid-dream by something touching her face. In the dream, Emily and her daughter Taylor were running through a field. The sun was beating down and it felt like summer. Taylor was falling behind, but still Emily kept running. She increased her pace and raced through the shoulder-high corn. She could hear Taylor's voice behind her. Her daughter was telling her to stop but Emily paid no attention to her. Taylor's cries faded away and then disappeared altogether.

That's when Emily had been disturbed and the events in the dream vanished from her mind. She wriggled her fingers and realised that she was able to move her hands. She must have struggled in her sleep and her bindings had come loose.

"Let's take a look at you, shall we?"
It was the man from the van – Luke. He removed the blindfold from Emily's face, and she was unable to see for a moment. Instinctively, she closed her eyes tight.
"No, no, no. That won't do. I need to inspect the product."
Emily could feel his breath on her cheek. He smelled of something sweet. She dared to open her eyes, and he was there, a few inches from her face. He was gazing into her eyes.

"The pupils will return to normal when they adjust to the light. There's some redness, but that's understandable. Do you use eyedrops?"

"Why are you doing this?" Emily said.

"Eyedrops?"

"Sometimes."

"We'll need their help now. The client has paid handsomely, and we have a reputation to uphold."

The sound of a door opening caused Luke to turn around.

"It's time."

This was the man with the German accent.

"I'm busy with her," Luke told him.

"I can take care of that. You're needed elsewhere. The van is outside waiting for you."

Luke turned back around to face Emily. "See you soon, beautiful."

The German walked over and, without warning he squirted something into Emily's left eye. He repeated the procedure with the right one. The liquid was cold, and it stung.

"The burning will pass. Those really are exquisite. I'm tempted to keep you for myself."

He took out a mobile phone and took some photographs.

"Exquisite. Are you hungry?"

"Please let me go," Emily said. "I have to go to my daughter."

"That's unfortunate. Would you like me to get you something to eat?"

"I want to go home."

"No, then. I'll give you something to help you sleep."

"Please," Emily said.

She knew exactly what that meant.

The German removed a syringe from inside his jacket and examined it. He shook it and held it in front of Emily's face.

"Sweet dreams."

Emily wriggled her left hand. It didn't take long to free it from the straps and the process was even quicker with the right hand. The needle of the syringe was placed against the inside of her arm, and the German man was staring directly into Emily's eyes again. She smiled at him, and he smiled back.

Then she summoned up as much saliva as she could muster and spat it into his eyes. His instincts kicked in and he placed a hand over his eyes. Emily knew he would – it was what she'd been taught. She had a temporary advantage and she used it. She gripped the hand holding the syringe and found the pressure point. Her nails dug deep and the fingers around the syringe opened. Emily took hold of it with her other hand, jammed the needle into the German's neck and pressed the plunger.

His eyes were still fixed to hers but the expression in them was changing rapidly. Emily released his hand, and he made no effort to fight. The drug worked quickly and he was powerless to stop it doing what it was designed to do. He collapsed to his knees and fell backwards, cracking his head on the concrete floor as he fell.

CHAPTER FORTY TWO

Emily took in the room. The walls and ceiling were white and it had a sterile aspect to it. There wasn't much inside. Apart from the chair she'd been sitting on, a single bed in the corner was all the room contained. The German on the floor wasn't moving. Emily looked closely and saw that he was still breathing. Some of her saliva had landed on his mouth and tiny bubbles of spit were moving in the corners.

She checked his jacket. All the pockets were empty. She did the same with the pockets of his trousers and took out a set of keys. She put these in her own pocket and got to her feet. An image of Taylor appeared in her mind's eye, and she held onto it. Her eight-year-old girl would be worried sick about her, and Emily could feel the skin on her face heating up. She looked at the German on the floor and kicked him hard in the temple. He didn't even flinch so she did it again.

Emily pulled open the door and stopped in the doorway to listen. Somebody coughed somewhere close by. Emily dared to venture into the corridor outside the room. It was dimly lit but Emily could see there were more doors on each side of it. The cough sounded again, and Emily made her way towards the source of it.

Kirsty Davies was lying on her back on the bed in the corner of the room. A drip was feeding something into her wrist. Emily made her way over. She stroked Kirsty's hair. "Can you hear me?"
Kirsty opened her eyes halfway and Emily knew straight away that she'd been drugged with something. The eyes were lifeless.

"I'm going to get you out of here," Emily told her.
There was nothing in Kirsty's eyes that told her she'd understood.
The eyelids closed again, and her breathing became heavy. Emily didn't think she was strong enough to get out of bed, let alone escape from

whatever hell they'd been taken to. She wondered if she would be able to carry her out, but Kirsty would be a dead weight, and Emily knew she wouldn't be able to get far.

"I'll come back for you," she said. "I'll get help, and I'll come back for you." Kirsty didn't respond. Emily placed a hand on her cheek, turned around and left the room.

The door at the end of the corridor was locked so Emily took out the German's keys and tried them, one by one. The last key she tried did the trick and Emily pushed the door open. She was now in some kind of reception area. The room was lit only by a subtle ceiling light and Emily could see a desk that could be a desk in any reception. It could be a doctor's waiting room or an accounting firm. The walls were covered in posters of luxury cars. Emily didn't pay them much attention. Her focus was on the only other door in the room, and she hoped and prayed that one of the six keys she had would open it.

She'd almost reached the door when a noise in the corridor made her freeze. It sounded like someone had slammed a door. Emily didn't wait to see who it was. She ran to the door and took out the keys. The first one she tried worked.

"Stop!" It was a woman's scream.
Emily opened the door just as the woman came inside the reception area. She moved with surprising speed, and she was across the room in no time. She reached for Emily, and she felt something scrape her arm. With all the strength she had left inside her, Emily shoved the woman away. She slammed the door, inserted the key and locked it behind her. Then she smacked the end of the key as hard as she could with her fist. The pain was intense, but it was worth it. The key was snapped in two, leaving the other half stuck inside the lock.

Emily didn't know if there was another way in or out of the building, but she wasn't going to stick around to find out. She ran. She ran like she had in the dream about the cornfield. She was in some kind of alleyway and the darkness made it hard to find her bearings. She could feel something on her arm – something warm and sticky, and when she placed her hand on the arm, she realised she'd been cut. Blood was trickling out of a wound on the forearm, and Emily was beginning to feel faint.

She reached the end of the alley and turned left. She had no idea where she was or where she was going but she knew she had to put as much distance between her and her temporary prison as she could. There was a peculiar tingling in her arm now and Emily didn't know what that meant.

There were no cars on the road and Emily wondered what time it was. She deduced it must be very late – perhaps it was the early hours of the morning. She was finding it difficult to walk and her legs were becoming numb. She stopped to catch her breath next to a row of rubbish bins but the stench of them was repulsive and she didn't stay there long.

A car engine could be heard somewhere in the distance, and it sounded like it was getting closer. Emily's eyelids were closing on their own and that's when she realised that she must have been drugged with something. That was what had scraped her arm during the scuffle with the mystery woman. Each step was now a real struggle, and she knew she wouldn't be able to carry on for much longer. The car engine was even closer.

Emily made her way back to the row of bins. She ignored the rancid odour and managed to crawl behind them. She could hear her heartbeat in her ears - the pulse was strangely hypnotic, and Emily felt herself drifting off to the beat of it. Her eyes closed but her other senses were still active. The funk coming from the bins seemed different now – it was sweeter somehow. Her ears picked up the noise of the car engine and then there was the sound of a door being slammed.

Emily managed to open her eyes, and she could see something on the road in front of the bins. It was a white Ford Transit van. The sound of voices told her there was more than one person there. The voices were replaced with the sound of footsteps and the last thing Emily was aware of was a pair of strong arms around her shoulders. She caught a glance of the van as she was helped into the passenger seat and that was it.

CHAPTER FORTY THREE

Smith was sleeping the sleep of the dead. It had been an extremely draining day and, with the help of a beer or six he'd fallen fast asleep as soon as Whitton had turned off the light. And that's why it took her longer than usual to wake him.

"Jason," she said for the fifth time. "Wake up."
Smith opened one eye. The room was pitch black.
"Where am I?" he said.
"Where do you think you are?" Whitton said. "You need to get up – they think Emily Grant has been found."
Smith was awake in an instant.

"The DI just called," Whitton said. "A woman matching her description was picked up by two men who work at the industrial estate in Murton. They were on their way home after a night shift and they spotted someone acting strangely."
"Is it definitely her?" Smith said.
He got out of bed and started getting dressed.
"The DI seems to think so. The woman they picked up was the same age, and she has the same eyes."
"Where is she now?"
"City Hospital," Whitton said. "The DI wants us to head straight there."

They were on the road in less than twenty minutes. Smith had woken Darren Lewis up and asked him to stay with Laura and Fran, and they'd set off for the hospital immediately.
"Where did they find her?" Smith asked.
"The DI didn't say," Whitton said.
"Do you think they let her go?"
"We don't know anything yet."

"Maybe she escaped."

"We'll know more when we speak to her," Whitton said. "There's no point in speculating until we've spoken to her."

"If it is definitely her, she'll be able to give us an idea where *The Workshop* is."

"We'll be at the hospital in five minutes," Whitton said. "We'll have some answers then."

"Can't you go any faster?"

"She's not going anywhere."

"I knew we should have taken my car," Smith said.

"You're still not insured," Whitton reminded him. "Just be patient."

"How can I be patient when there's a woman with the potential to end this, and you're driving like an old lady?"

Whitton didn't comment on this, but the expression on her face told a story of its own.

"I'm sorry," Smith said after a moment of silence had passed. "This could be the break we've waited for."

DI Smyth was waiting for them in the waiting area of the hospital. He introduced them to a young woman with dyed white hair. Her name was Gloria Floyd, and she was the doctor who had attended to the woman when she was first brought in.

"How is she?" Smith asked.

"She was very weak when she arrived," Dr Floyd said. "She was dehydrated and somewhat delirious. We're getting her fluids back to normal and I've given her a sedative to help her rest."

"Did she say anything when she came in?" Whitton said.

"She was in no state. Your DI has explained the seriousness of the situation, but I have to make the welfare of the patient my main priority."

"It's highly likely the woman who was brought in holds the welfare of another woman in her hands and it's imperative that we speak to her as soon as possible," Smith explained.

"She is in no state right now," Dr Floyd said. "You'll be able to talk to her in the morning."

Something occurred to Smith.

"Is it definitely her? Is it definitely Emily Grant?"

"No doubt about it," DI Smyth said. "The odds on a woman of the same age having identical eyes are astronomical."

"I've come across heterochromia before," Dr Floyd said. "But this is the most unusual case I've ever seen."

"Does her daughter know?" Smith asked. "Does Taylor know that her mother is OK? I promised her that her mum would be fine. She needs to be told."

"Relax," DI Smyth said. "Mrs Grant's parents and daughter have been informed."

"Where are the men who found her?" Smith said. "Please tell me you didn't let them leave."

"Baldwin and PC Miller are with them now. Dr Floyd has kindly allowed us to use her office."

"I want to talk to them," Smith said.

"Naturally."

"But I need a smoke first," Smith said. "I'll be back in five minutes."

"Is he always like this?" Dr Floyd asked Whitton.

"Like what?" she said.

"So wound up."

"He tends to take things a bit personally sometimes," Whitton explained.

"It's his worst trait," DI Smyth said. "And it's also his biggest asset at times."

"I imagine he must be very good at what he does," Dr Floyd said.

"He is," DI Smyth admitted. "He's aged me in the time I've had the pleasure of working with him, but I wouldn't have it any other way."

"Do you have any idea what could have happened to her?" Whitton asked Dr Floyd.

"I believe she was drugged. She had a wound on her arm that was consistent with a needle puncture. I think the needle scraped the skin and she wasn't given a full dose of whatever it was that was in the syringe. Without carrying out a tox analysis, it's impossible to say what drug she was injected with, but I suspect some kind of tranquilizer was used. If you'll excuse me now – my shift ended over an hour ago, and I need some sleep."

"Thank you for your help," DI Smyth said. "We really appreciate it."

Dr Floyd smiled at him. "One of my colleagues will be in touch as soon as Mrs Grant is well enough to talk to you. I'm sure DS Smith will want to be the first to know."

CHAPTER FORTY FOUR

Smith and DI Smyth went inside the office that Dr Floyd shared with two other doctors. Baldwin and PC Miller were sitting opposite two men who looked to be in their mid-thirties. Whitton had gone home. She'd received a phone call from Lucy telling her that both Laura and Fran weren't feeling well. They'd been sick and Lucy thought they both had a mild fever. DI Smyth had told her to go. He offered to give Smith a lift home when they were finished at the hospital.

PC Miller stood up when the two detectives came in.
"Morning, sir," he said to DI Smyth. "This is Jack Norman and his brother Steven. They've given us the location of where they found her, but we thought it would be best to wait for you to get here before they were interviewed about anything else."
"That's fine," DI Smyth said. "You can leave us to it, thanks."
PC Miller nodded and left the room.
"Do you want me to go too?" Baldwin said.
"You can stay," Smith decided.

"Have you been offered anything to drink?" DI Smyth asked the two brothers.
"We got a couple of cokes from the machine," the taller of the two told him. "I'm Jack – the good looking one."
"In your dreams, mate," his brother said.
"We really appreciate you sticking around," Smith said.
"It's fine," Jack said. "I could see she'd been mistreated, and I knew the police would want to speak to us."
"We're not due back on shift until Monday anyway," Steven added.
"Can you talk us through what happened?" said DI Smyth.
"We left the warehouse just after three," Jack said.

"That's an odd time to finish work," Smith said.

"We were supposed to finish at ten last night," Steven said. "But one of the conveyors packed in, and it took a while to fix."

"We're always up for a bit of overtime anyway," Jack said. "Money's tight these days, isn't it?"

Smith didn't comment on this.

"Where is the warehouse you work in?" he asked instead.

"In the industrial estate in Murton."

"What company is it?"

"What has that got to do with anything?" Jack said.

Smith ignored the question. "What's the name of the company you work for?"

"Jones' Logistics," Steven replied for him.

"I don't think that's important," DI Smyth said.

Smith shrugged his shoulders.

"Where did you spot the woman?" DI Smyth said.

"Just off Murton Way," Jack said. "Our Steven saw her first. I was driving, and we both thought it was a strange place to be wandering around."

"There's not much there," Steven said. "No clubs or pubs, and no residential estates."

"We gave the exact location to the other officers," Jack said.

"What did you do when you spotted her?" Smith said.

"I stopped the van of course," Jack said. "I knew there was something wrong."

"How did you know that?"

"Because she was all over the place. And it looked like she was trying to hide."

"Could you elaborate on that?" DI Smyth said.

"She stopped by the bins on Beckett Avenue," Jack said. "She kept walking and then she walked back to where she'd just come from."

"She was barely conscious when we found her," Steven said. "And her pulse was very weak. I knew we needed to get her to a hospital."

"Our Steven is the safety officer at the warehouse," Jack said.

"I know advanced first aid," Steven added.

"What did you do then?" DI Smyth said.

"We picked her up and helped her inside the van. It was a bit of a squeeze, three of us in the front, but we managed."

"You were in a van?" Smith said.

"Got it a couple of years ago," Jack said. "We do the odd removal job when we're not working at the warehouse. Like I said, money's tight and the odd extra comes in handy. It's all above board – the taxman knows all about it."

Smith couldn't care less about that.

"Did you see anyone else around when you found the woman?" he said.

"Not a soul," Jack said. "There never is anyone around at that time of night."

"Do you make a habit of driving around in the early hours of the morning?"

"Only when a shift runs over," Steven said. "Are you accusing us of something now?"

"We didn't have to stick around waiting for you to get out of bed," Jack said. "We were both actually looking forward to getting our heads down in our own beds."

"My colleague didn't mean anything by it," DI Smyth said. "And we really do appreciate your time."

"Is she going to be alright?" Steven said. "She was in a bad way when we picked her up."

"She'll be fine," DI Smyth said.

"Did you see her eyes?" Jack said.

"We haven't been able to get in to see her yet," Smith said.

"Really unusual eyes," Jack said. "She probably could be a model. Is she?"

"I don't know," Smith said. "I don't think so."

"Do you think they'll let me come and see her when she's well enough?"

"Why would you want to do that?"

"Just to make sure she's alright," Jack said.

"We've got your contact details," DI Smyth said. "Someone will be in touch anyway to arrange a convenient time for you to come in and make a statement."

"And I'm sure she'll be more concerned about seeing her daughter," Smith said. "Rather than someone from her fan club."

"What is your problem?"

"How long have you got?" Smith said.

"I think we've covered everything for now," DI Smyth said. "Thank you again for what you did."

Jack stood up. "Any time. I think your mate there should think about working on his people skills. He should be grateful for what we did, not treating us like we're the criminals."

"We'll be in touch," DI Smyth said.

CHAPTER FORTY FIVE

"Are you going to tell me what the hell that was all about?" DI Smyth said. He and Smith were walking back to the waiting area of the hospital.

"What was what all about?" Smith said.

"Those men deserve a medal," DI Smyth said. "And you all but interrogated them as though they were suspects."

"I didn't like them," Smith said. "Especially the older one."

"They probably saved Emily Grant's life tonight, and you treated them like dirt."

"I suppose I was a bit hard on them," Smith said. "But the van thing stirred up something inside me."

"Van thing?"

"Come on, boss," Smith said. "Don't you think it's a bit of a coincidence that a white van has been seen in places where two of the victims were last seen and another victim happens to be rescued by two men in a white van?"

"You can't possible believe the Norman brothers are involved?"

"I don't know what to believe."

"Think about it," DI Smyth said. "If they do work at *The Workshop*, why bring Emily here? They would have taken her straight back to where she was being held prisoner. You're not thinking rationally."

"I want a police presence outside Emily's room," Smith said, out of the blue.

"What for?" DI Smyth said.

"Because there's a chance that she could still be in danger."

"How did you come to that conclusion?"

"I don't know," Smith said. "It's just a feeling in my gut. Something is telling me that Emily's escape isn't the end of it. What's to stop them coming here and finishing what they started?"

"Besides a hospital full of people, you mean? I think you need to go home and get some more sleep. Emily isn't going anywhere."

"I'm staying here. If you won't authorise some uniform to babysit her, I'll do it myself."

"You'll do no such thing," DI Smyth said. "I need you fully alert tomorrow – I mean later today. If it means so much to you, I'll arrange something with the hospital. See if they can keep a close watch on her room. We only have a few more hours before it gets light, so I suggest we get out of here."

He headed for the exit, leaving Smith with no option but to follow him.

"Billie thinks she recognised the skirt the dead teenage girl was wearing when she was found," DI Smyth said.

They'd just exited the car park of the hospital.

"She reckons it's part of the uniform of an all-girls school in Heworth – Heworth High. Billie's sister attended the school a few years ago and the skirt isn't something you can buy in any shop. It has to be specially ordered."

"If that's the case," Smith said. "It should be pretty easy to get an ID for the girl. Why has nobody reported her missing?"

"We don't know," DI Smyth said. "We'll be following it up first thing."

"Why chop off her hands and feet?" Smith wondered out loud. "What possible reason would they have for doing that? Surely nobody would be so sick and twisted that they'd put in an order for a teenage girl's hands and feet."

"Webber believes the answer to that will become apparent when we have an ID for the girl."

"We're getting closer," Smith said. "Emily Grant's escape is going to be the break we've been waiting for. I wonder how she managed it."

"You'll get the chance to ask her that tomorrow."

"Where do I stand with the accident with the police car?" Smith changed the subject. "From a legal perspective, I mean."

"I thought you were a police officer," DI Smyth said. "With a background in law."

"That bit of the law is a bit hazy. I let my insurance lapse for a month, so technically the vehicle wasn't covered when Darren had the accident."

"It's possible you could argue that it was an unintentional lapse, and a month is a relatively short period of time. As far as I recall, driving without insurance is one of the few road traffic offences where the burden of proof lies entirely with the defendant."

"Darren is worried that he's going to get points on his license," Smith said.

"I don't think that will happen. It was an accident – he has a valid license, and he wasn't aware that the vehicle wasn't insured."

"But surely, that puts it all on me."

"Technically," DI Smyth confirmed. "But it looks to me like a pretty open and shut case, and I don't think the penalties will be too harsh. You'll probably get away with the mandatory penalty which is usually a fine of a few hundred pounds."

"I can live with that," Smith said.

"Just get your damn insurance sorted out."

"Yes, boss."

"And don't even think about driving the car again until you do."

DI Smyth stopped outside Smith's house.

"Thanks for the lift," Smith said. "I'm going to head straight for the hospital tomorrow."

"I thought you might say that," DI Smyth said. "Get a few hours' sleep."

"We're going to make progress tomorrow."

DI Smyth nodded and pulled away from the kerb.

The lights were on inside the house when Smith went inside. He found Whitton in the kitchen with Darren Lewis.

"What's going on?" he asked. "How are the girls?"

"Lucy's upstairs with them now," Whitton said. "We've managed to get their temperatures down, and they're both asleep."

"What do you think is wrong with them?"

"Apparently, there's a bug going around at the school. I've given them something to get the fever down and I think they should stay off school for a few days. I'm sure they'll be fine."

"Where's Andrew?" Smith asked Darren. "You didn't leave him by himself next door, did you?"

Darren nodded to the baby monitor on the table. "I'll hear him if he wakes up."

Right on cue the sound of gurgling came over the speaker. This was followed by a string of indecipherable words. Andrew was engaged in a conversation with himself.

"I'd better get back next door," Darren said.

He picked up the baby monitor. Andrew was still talking to himself.

"He sounds like my husband after a good night out," Whitton said.

Darren laughed. "I'll see you tomorrow."

"I'm going outside for a quick smoke before I hit the sack," Smith said,

He didn't know then that a few miles away, a group of people were hastily trying to cover their tracks in a building where four people had lost their lives in the past week. These people were pros, and they were already in the process of putting one of their many contingency plans in place. The original *Workshop* was no more, but that meant nothing. As long as there were perverted individuals with big enough bank balances, it would be business as usual until someone told them otherwise.

CHAPTER FORTY SIX

The morning of the first day of October dawned grey and damp. Smith woke before his alarm and the bedroom was pitch black even though the sun was supposed to have risen already. A glance at his phone told him it was just before half-seven. Whitton was still fast asleep in the bed next to him and Smith left her there. It had been past four when they'd finally managed to get to bed and both of them knew that today was going to be a draining one.

Smith went downstairs and switched on the light in the kitchen. The sun was fighting a losing battle with thick grey clouds that seemed dangerously close to the ground. Smith opened the back door, and the smell of impending rain hit his nostrils. He wasn't a big fan of days like these, and he knew there was very slim chance of the cloud cover moving off anytime soon. He lit a cigarette, and the first drops of rain started to fall. He finished the cigarette quickly and went back inside to make some coffee.

While the kettle was boiling, he checked his phone and saw there were three new messages. He was relieved to see that one of them was from his insurance company. After clicking on the link, Smith followed the instructions, and he'd renewed his car insurance before the kettle had even boiled. He cursed himself for being such an idiot. It really was a simple process, and he wished he'd done it sooner.

Whitton came in shortly afterwards.
"I've sorted out the car insurance," Smith told her. "The Sierra is officially legal again."
"Better late than never," Whitton said. "Has the kettle just boiled?"
"I'll make it," Smith offered. "It looks like it's going to be a shitty day."
"Yorkshire in October."
Smith made her some coffee. "Have you checked on the girls?"

"They're fast asleep," Whitton said. "I felt their foreheads and they're still a bit hot, but it doesn't seem to be as bad as it was. They can stay off school today. It's Friday, so they're not going to miss much."

"I'm going to go straight to the hospital," Smith said. "Emily Grant should be up to talking to us and we need to see what she remembers about what happened to her."

Whitton sipped her coffee. "I couldn't get straight to sleep last night, and something occurred to me. If Emily managed to escape, they're going to be rattled, aren't they?"

"I thought about that too," Smith said. "I offered to stay outside her room last night, but the boss wouldn't have it. He arranged for extra hospital security."

"I suppose they'd be taking a huge chance trying anything at the hospital."

"It's happened before," Smith said. "It's surprisingly easy to gain access to a hospital room. The DI made sure the hospital is aware of the risk and I got the impression that they took it seriously. I suppose I should think about heading over there."

* * *

Emily Grant was experiencing a strong sense of déjà vu. She'd woken from a deep sleep to find herself in an unfamiliar room, and for a second, she wondered if she was back in the place she'd been strapped to the chair. She took a moment to take in her surroundings. She was on a bed and when she moved, she realised that she was free to do so. A tube was feeding something into her wrist from an IV drip next to the bed. She was aware of sounds outside the room, and she realised that she was in a hospital.

She managed to sit up in the bed and when she glanced to the side she saw that there was a bottle of water on the table next to the bed. She opened it and took a long drink. The door opened and Emily froze. A man came inside the room and approached the bed. He looked young and he was unfamiliar. He was wearing some kind of security uniform. He definitely wasn't one of the people who had held her captive.

"How are you feeling?" he asked.

"Where am I?" Emily said.

"City Hospital. You were brought in last night. Can you remember that?"

"I think so."

"The police will want to talk to you later this morning. Is there anything you need? Are you in any pain?"

"Are you a doctor?" Emily said.

He laughed. "Hospital security. I volunteered to stand sentry outside the room all night. The name's Keith."

"You stood outside all night?"

Keith held up his hands. "Busted. OK, I had a chair to sit on, but I was out there."

"I don't know whether to feel privileged or terrified," Emily said. "I didn't think City Hospital had that kind of resources."

"Don't get too big headed," Keith said. "I'd already finished my shift, and I offered to stay on for a few hours. I wasn't even paid for it."

Emily smiled at him. "My hero."

"You have the most amazing eyes," Keith said. "Sorry – I bet you get that all the time."

"You could say that," Emily said. "I have a rare condition called heterochromia. I was born with two different coloured eyes. My daughter has the same condition. Oh my God. Taylor – does she know where I am?"

"I don't know."

"Could you find out for me?"

"Of course," Keith said. "I'll go and find someone to help."

He left the room and didn't come back. After a few minutes the door opened, and a man and a woman came in. The woman looked to be in her forties and she was wearing a nurses' uniform. The man was a bit younger and he was dressed in a pair of jeans and a Led Zeppelin T-Shirt.

"How are you feeling?" It was the man.

He introduced himself as Detective Sergeant Jason Smith and he told her he was very much looking forward to talking to her.

CHAPTER FORTY SEVEN

Smith waited for the nurse to finish her routine check and leave them alone and pulled up a chair next to the bed.

He took out his phone and placed it on the table next to the bed. "Do you mind if I record the conversation?"

Whitton had suggested this. She told Smith that whatever Emily told him needed to be documented and Smith had agreed. He would play the recording to the rest of the team afterwards.

Emily had no problem with this. Smith turned on the voice recorder and made sure it was working properly.

"How are you doing?"

"I feel confused," Emily said. "It's like I've had a terrible nightmare and I'm not quite sure if I'm still dreaming or not."

"You're safe now," Smith said.

"What happened to the security bloke?"

"He's gone home."

"Do you know he stayed outside all night when he didn't have to?" Emily said. "He wasn't paid for it."

"Resources are tight everywhere," Smith said. "We have the same problem in the police."

"He didn't have to do that though."

"There are still plenty of good people in this city," Smith said.

"I must get his details. I want to thank him properly."

"Do you remember being brought here last night?" Smith said.

"I remember bits and pieces. I remember a white van and two people and then the bright lights of the hospital. I thought... Oh my God, I really thought..."

"What did you think, Emily?"

"It was the same as before. There was a white van there too."

"I understand this is hard," Smith said. "But I really need you to tell me everything. You took Taylor to her ballet class on Wednesday evening. Is that right?"

"She was so excited. She was going to perform a recital she'd spent hours practicing. Does she know? Does Taylor know where I am? Keith said he would find out."

"Taylor knows," Smith confirmed. "She's safe and sound at your parents' house, and she'll be coming to see you later. You should be very proud of her - it was Taylor who phoned Katie when you didn't come and pick her up after class. She's a very special young lady."

The door to the room opened and Dr Floyd came inside the room.

"I thought you might be here," she said to Smith.

He paused the recording.

"Don't you sleep?" he asked her.

"I could say the same thing about you. I just need to check a few things, and I'll leave you in peace."

"When will I be able to go home?" Emily said.

"I'd like to keep you in for at least another night," Dr Floyd said. "Just to be on the safe side. We still don't know what you were sedated with, and I want to keep an eye on any possible side effects."

Smith resumed the recording as soon as Dr Floyd had gone.

"Can you talk me through what you remember after dropping Taylor off at her ballet class?"

"I set off for Katie's house," Emily said. "Like I always do. There was a white van parked on her road."

"I don't suppose you can remember the registration plates?"

"I'm sorry, I can't."

"It's fine," Smith said. "It was a long shot. Who goes around remembering number plates?"

"A man got out," Emily said. "He was looking at his phone and he looked really frustrated. When I got closer, I was sure I recognised him."

"Could you describe him?" Smith said.

"He wasn't very old. Perhaps in his early twenties, and he had a friendly face. He was average height – not as tall as you, and he had short brown hair. He introduced himself as Luke. He told me his GPS wasn't working properly, and he mentioned the road he was looking for. He wasn't far away so I gave him directions."

"What happened then? Did he get back in the van?"

"He told me I have amazing eyes," Emily said. "I get that a lot, so I didn't think much of it, but then he asked if he could take a photograph."

"Didn't you think that was odd?"

"That's happened a few times before too. He looked harmless enough. He asked me to stand against the van and he pretended to take photos."

"Pretended?" Smith said.

"When he showed me the screen there was nothing on it. Then he tapped on the van and before I knew it the door opened and people were grabbing me. It all happened so fast. I tried to scream but someone had put a hand over my mouth. That's all I remember apart from the Anais Anais."

"Anais Anais?" Smith repeated.

"It's a perfume," Emily said. "My mum wears it."

"And you could smell that inside the van?"

"I'm sure of it. I don't remember much after that – I think they drugged me, but I'm sure about the perfume."

Something occurred to Smith. It was something Taylor had told him. Emily's daughter had mentioned a man with a friendly face during the walk to the ballet class. He asked Emily about it. She looked right at him and her blue eye seemed to brighten somehow.

"That's where I recognised him from. I knew I'd seen him before."

"Do you know this man?" Smith said.

"Only in passing. I'd never spoken to him before. Like I said, he told me his name was Luke."

"We have reason to believe he'd been following you for quite some time," Smith said.

"That's really creepy."

"We're going to catch these people," Smith said. "That's a promise."

He realised that this was the second time he'd made a promise he had no idea he would be able to keep, and he made a mental note to stop doing that.

Emily reached for the bottle of water. She opened it and took a drink. Her eyes found Smith's again. "There was another woman there with me."

"Where are you talking about?" Smith said.

"Wherever it was they took me. She mentioned someone called Luke too."

"Was her name Kirsty Davies?"

"That's right," Emily said. "She's still there. I promised her I would come back for her."

CHAPTER FORTY EIGHT

"Are you feeling up to carrying on?" Smith said.
Emily Grant had started to sob after talking about Kirsty. She'd cried for quite some time and Smith hadn't stopped her.

Emily nodded and blew her nose with a tissue.
"I promised. I said I'd help her."
"And that's what you're doing now,' Smith said. "The more you tell us about the place they took you to the better chance we have of finding out where it is. You were forced into the van on Wednesday. They drugged you and they took you somewhere. What do you remember about when you woke up?"
"I didn't know where I was," Emily said. "And my first thoughts were of Taylor. I called out for her, and I heard a woman telling me to be quiet. It was Kirsty. She said they could hear us."
"What do you think she meant by that?"
"I don't know. She told me to keep my voice down, and she told me she'd been taken too. Then she mentioned Luke. I think he was the one who took her. I panicked and the only thing I could think of to do was scream. The next time I woke up I was somewhere else, and Kirsty wasn't there anymore."

Dr Lloyd came back in.
"I think Emily has had enough for now. She needs to rest."
"I need to ask some more questions," Smith said. "This is extremely important."
"It's also important that Emily gets her rest."
"I'm fine," Emily said. "I have to help Kirsty."
Dr Lloyd's puzzled expression told them she had no idea who Kirsty was, but she didn't press further.
"Only if you're sure," she said.

"I'm sure," Emily said.

"You said you woke up somewhere else," Smith said.

"I could feel it," Emily said. "They'd put a blindfold over my eyes, but I just sensed I was in a different room. I was still strapped to the chair, but I was alone."

"They strapped you to a chair?"

Emily nodded. "But the bindings had loosened. I had a bad dream, and I must have struggled in my sleep."

"Did you manage to free yourself?" Smith said.

"Not at first. Someone was touching my face and when the blindfold was removed, I saw it was Luke. He was really gentle."

Smith didn't know how to feel about this.

"What did he do?" he asked.

"He said I needed eyedrops to relieve the redness in my eyes and then he said something really creepy. He told me the client had paid handsomely, and they had a reputation to uphold. What did he mean by that?"

"I really don't know," Smith lied.

"Then the door opened, and the German came into the room."

"German?"

"I'm sure his accent was German."

"Can you describe him?"

"Older than Luke," Emily said. "Thinning hair and there was something weird about him. Like he was enjoying keeping me captive. He said he was tempted to keep me for himself like I was some kind of pet."

"Did he hurt you?" Smith said.

Emily started to laugh, and it caught Smith off guard.

"Sorry," she said. "No, he didn't hurt me. He told Luke he would take over. He said Luke had work to do – the van was waiting for him outside. Then he asked me if I was hungry and when I said I wasn't he told me he was going to make me sleep again. That's when I really knew I had to get out of there."

"I'm still trying to figure out how you did it."

"The straps binding me to the chair were easy enough to get out of," Emily said. "And then my self-defence classes kicked in. I could see the syringe he was holding, and I knew what he was going to do so I smiled at him."

"You did what?"

"I smiled at him," Emily said. "These eyes have their uses, and he smiled back. That's when I spat right in his eyes. You do that and you incapacitate your attacker for a few seconds. It's almost impossible to think about anything else. He wiped his eyes, and I grabbed the hand holding the syringe. There's a pressure point on the wrist that acts like an off switch for the fingers. He lost his grip on the syringe - I grabbed it and stuck it in his neck. He was on the floor in seconds."

"That is truly amazing," Smith said. "Remind me not to get on the wrong side of you."

Emily smiled at him. "Oh, and I might have kicked him in the head a couple of times when he was down."

"You should have kicked him more times," Smith said. "But I will definitely remember not to piss you off."

"I found Kirsty in another room" Emily carried on. "I managed to get hold of the German's keys and I found her in a bed further down the corridor. She was in a bad way and there was no way I would be able to get her out of there with me. I promised her I would get help. Another door led to what looked like a reception area."

"Can you describe it?" Smith said.

"It was like any other reception. Big desk, and a few chairs. And there were pictures of cars on the walls – expensive looking cars. I managed to get outside by unlocking another door but not before a woman tried to stop me."

"What did she do?"

"She came at me with what I later learned was a syringe. She must have got me but luckily, I didn't get the full dose. I fought her off, slammed the door and locked it from the other side. Then I made sure she couldn't open it with her own key by snapping the key inside the lock."

Smith couldn't believe what the woman with the unusual eyes was telling him. You really couldn't make this stuff up.

"What did you do then?" he asked.

"I ran," Emily said. "I didn't care where I ran to, but I knew I had to get away. But then the drug must have started to work because I found it hard to move my legs. I managed to crawl behind some bins and the last thing I remember is the van. I thought they'd found me again."

"But they didn't," Smith said. "That is a remarkable story, and it's quite possible you'll be able to help us find these people. I know you're exhausted, but I'd like you to work with someone who has a much better grasp of the geography of the city than I do. We know where you were found, and it's possible we'll be able to pinpoint the location of the place you were held captive by working back from there. Do you reckon you can help us with that?"

"Of course," Emily said without thinking.

"And I think it might help for you to work with a police artist. It might give us a better idea of what this Luke character looks like."

"I can do that."

"You really are an amazing woman, Emily," Smith said. "And I'm not just referring to your eyes. I'll let you get some rest. Someone will be in later to see if they can help you retrace the route you took."

CHAPTER FORTY NINE

"There is a Luke Nelson on the list of people who've donated blood at the university in the past six months," DI Smyth began the morning briefing.
"Bring him in immediately," Smith said.
He'd just got back from the hospital with the recording of the interview of the decade.
"Hold your horses," DI Smyth said.
"No," Smith said. "Emily Grant mentioned someone called Luke and she also said Kirsty Davies talked about a Luke. What more do you need?"
"If you'd let me finish," DI Smyth said. "We've been unable to locate Mr Nelson at present. He's not answering his phone and the uniforms who went to his address couldn't find anyone at home. There is a vehicle registered in his name, and I've issued a BOLO. If he's in the city we'll find him."
"I apologise," Smith offered.

"I have every confidence that we will find Mr Nelson before the end of the day," DI Smyth said. "As you all know two more bodies were found last night. It was a man and a teenage girl, and we might have a clue about the identity of the girl. Billie Jones recognised the skirt she was wearing. It's the skirt the students at the all-girls school in Heworth wear. I've sent some uniforms to the school, and we'll know if any of their students happen to be missing. Moving on to Emily Grant – I can see from the expression on Smith's face that he came up trumps at the hospital."
"You're not wrong there, boss," Smith said. "I've arranged for someone to go through a map of the city with her to see if they can narrow down the place she was held captive, and I've also asked her to work with a police artist, but I want you listen to the chat I had with her. I have to warn you, it's like something out of an action film. Mrs Grant is a truly exceptional woman."

He took out his phone. "Is there any way to make this louder? My phone's speaker isn't the best."

It took DC Moore no time at all to connect Smith's phone to the speakers at the back of the room. Smith started the recording, and everyone settled down to listen to it.

A few minutes later, the final words of the voice recording sounded and there was absolute silence inside the small conference room. Bridge was the first to find his voice.

"Who is this lady?" he said. "Superwoman?"

"Someone you really don't want to meet in a dark alley at night," DC Moore added.

"She's done self-defence classes," Smith explained. "And I for one am glad she did. She escaped from *The Workshop*, and she's going to lead us right to it."

"How long do you think it'll take to get a rough location?" DC King said.

"It shouldn't take too long. From what I can gather, the sedative these people use acts quickly, so I don't think *The Workshop* is too far from where Emily was found. We're getting so close – I can feel it."

"Does anyone have any thoughts to share after listening to that?" DI Smyth said.

"It basically confirms what we suspected about the victims being followed beforehand," Whitton said.

DC King nodded. "And Emily's daughter said this Luke character had been keeping an eye on them for quite some time."

"They do a lot of homework before striking," Smith said. "This is a highly organised team of people."

"They must have access to drugs," DC Moore said. "And other medical equipment."

"We don't know if the actual surgeries are carried out at the place they're taken to, do we?" Bridge said.

"I think they are," Smith said. "Why go to all the trouble of abducting someone and transporting them somewhere if you have to take them somewhere else afterwards? I reckon they'll have some kind of operating theatre on the premises."

"Anything else?" DI Smyth said.

"She mentioned a row of bins," DC Moore said. "That ought to help us."

"We already know where the bins are, Harry," Smith reminded him. "It's where she was found, and that's going to be the starting point when we work backwards."

"Sorry, Sarge," DC Moore said. "I was thinking out loud again."

"We know there are at least three of them," Bridge said. "The man called Luke, the German and the woman who tried to stop Emily from escaping."

"The German," DC King said. "Emily said she gave him a dose of sedative and a couple of kicks to the head."

"What's your point?" DC Moore said.

"It's possible he's going to be out of action for a while."

"I still don't know why that matters."

"It probably doesn't," Smith said. "But I know for a fact that they'll be shitting in their pants right now. One of their victims was able to escape and that wasn't part of the plan."

"Do you think they might go to ground?" DC Moore said.

"They're not stupid," Smith said. "There's every chance that they might decide to run but that's not so easy when they still have paying clients waiting for their products. And you do not clear out a hospital in a hurry, no matter how makeshift that hospital is."

"Especially in broad daylight," DC King said.

"They've taken someone else," Whitton said.

Everyone turned to look at her.

"Emily said something about the German coming in to take over from Luke," Whitton explained. "Luke had work to do, which can be translated as him heading out to take another victim."

"You're absolutely right," Smith said. "They've taken someone else and unless we find them, God knows what they're going to do to them. Fuck."

"Can we listen to the recording again?" Bridge said.

"Has something occurred to you?" DI Smyth said.

"I don't know – there was something in it that sounded some alarm bells, but I can't for the life of me figure out what it is."

Smith started the recording from the beginning again. He watched Bridge's face the whole time but if he was expecting to see a spark of recognition it didn't materialise.

"Well?" he said when it was finished.

Bridge frowned so hard the lines on his forehead made him look a decade older than he was.

"I think I might know where *The Workshop* is."

CHAPTER FIFTY

"Something doesn't feel right about this, boss," Smith said.

"Why do you always have to say things like that at times like these?" DI Smyth said.

"I don't know – it feels wrong. It's too convenient."

"Look at the evidence. The row of bins where Emily Grant was found is a stones' throw from the offices of Artemis Trading. She described the reception area and Bridge said it's exactly what the Artemis Trading reception looks like."

"It still feels iffy to me," Smith said. "Horace Nagel just happens to introduce me to a bloke who hands me the name of the company on a plate. Then they sail off into the distance after making a complete fool out of me. Don't you see how suspicious that is?"

"What is your problem?" DI Smyth said. "Why do you always insist on making things more complicated than they are?"

"You're wrong about Artemis Trading."

"The raid on the office is going ahead," DI Smyth said.

"When is it happening?"

"As soon as the warrant is procured. It's taking longer than I hoped."

DC Moore came inside DI Smyth's office.

"Can I have a word?"

"What is it?" DI Smyth said.

DC Moore handed him a piece of paper. "This makes for interesting reading. It's a list of the board of directors of Artemis Trading, as well as the main players in the company itself. Take a look at the CEO."

"Gerald Nelson," DI Smyth read.

"Ring any bells?" DC Moore said.

"Not particularly."

"Who is he?" Smith asked.

"Gerald Nelson is not only the Chief Executive Officer of Artemis Trading," DC Moore said. "He also happens to be Luke Nelson's father."

"How did you find this out?" DI Smyth said.

"Facebook, sir. Luke's security is virtually non-existent and there are a few photos with him and his father."

"That's very interesting."

"No, it isn't," Smith said. "It stinks of something."

"If you tell me, it's too much of a coincidence," DI Smyth said. "I will physically escort you out of this office right now."

"Hear me out," Smith said. "We've got a bloke called Luke who's on the list of people donating blood. Kirsty Davies was abducted right after giving blood, and it took us all of five minutes to come to that conclusion. Emily Grant told us that this Luke offered his name pretty much straight away. We now know the Luke who gave blood is the son of the man at the helm of a company mentioned by a known criminal. These people are pros, boss – they know exactly how we operate, and they would not make a balls-up like this. And who has no security on their social media these days? No, this is definitely suspicious."

DI Smyth's phone started to ring on the desk. He picked it up so quickly that Smith flinched.

"DI Smyth."

Smith watched as he listened for a moment.

"Thank you," he said. "We'll be right there."

"I assume we've got the warrant for the wild goose chase," Smith dared.

"You'll see," DI Smyth said. "You'll see. I want to do this properly and I'm not taking any chances. We don't know if these people are armed, but I'm working on the assumption that they are. You know the drill."

Smith did. "The armed unit will go in first. And we'll stand back and wait for them to come out and tell us they've found fuck all."

"Enough," DI Smyth said. "That's enough. You're excused. Go and grab some coffee – smoke a cigarette, just get out of here."

Smith stood up. "With pleasure. I take it my presence isn't required at Artemis Trading."

"Get lost," DI Smyth said. "Get out before I do something we'll both later come to regret."

Smith walked down the corridor and headed for the exit. He was stopped by PC Baldwin by the front desk.

"We've got an ID for the teenage girl, Sarge."

"Who is she?" Smith said.

"Her name is Stacey Madison. She's a student at Heworth High."

"Why wasn't she reported missing?" Smith said.

"Typical teenage stuff," Baldwin said. "Her parents thought she was staying over at a friend's house, so they didn't think anything of it."

"What about the friend? Why didn't the friend suspect anything? Or the school for that matter."

"The school thought she was off sick," Baldwin said. "And the friend told the officers who spoke to her that Stacey was really at her boyfriend's place, and it was normal for her not to get in touch while she was with her boyfriend. It was a cunning teenage plan that backfired in the worst possible way."

"Has anyone spoken to the boyfriend?"

"He's devastated, Sarge. And he had no idea that Stacey was missing."

"I don't buy it," Smith said. "If they planned for her to stay over with him, why didn't he think it was odd when she didn't show up?"

"Apparently she sent him a message to say she wasn't coming."

"Why did they take her?" Smith said. "Why was she taken to *The Workshop*?"

"According to her best friend," Baldwin said. "Stacey had something called polydactyly. It's where someone is born with extra fingers or toes, and in Stacey's case she had six toes on each foot and six fingers on each of her hands. It's extremely rare."

"That's why her hands and feet were chopped off," Smith said. "This just makes me feel more and more ill every day."

"It is very disturbing."

Smith nodded and walked towards the exit. He stopped in the doorway and turned around.

"Stacey didn't send that message."

"Sarge?" Baldwin said.

"It was sent from her phone," Smith said. "But Stacey didn't write it. You still have a contact who can fast-track phone records, don't you?"

"Not officially."

"I don't care whether it's above board or not," Smith said. "Get hold of Stacey's service provider and see if your contact can pinpoint where the phone was when that message was sent."

"I'll get onto it right away."

"Thanks, Baldwin," Smith said. "If anybody's looking for me tell them you have no idea where I am."

CHAPTER FIFTY ONE

If Bridge were to describe the expression on the face of the receptionist at Artemis Trading, he would use adjectives like *bewildered* and *perplexed*. The man looked utterly gobsmacked when Bridge and the team went in after being given the green light from the armed unit.

It was exactly as Smith had suspected – there was nothing inside the building that housed the offices of Artemis Trading other than what you would expect to find in an office building. There was no evidence that anyone had been held captive and butchered inside. It was an office building, nothing more and nothing less.

As luck would have it, Gerald Nelson was on the premises when it was raided. Gerald was justifiably furious, and he threatened York Police with legal action more than once. DI Smyth managed to calm him down sufficiently to be able to discuss the matter inside his office. He apologised for the inconvenience but explained that there were some things that needed clearing up.

Gerald didn't offer him anything to drink. The angry CEO told him to make it quick and DI Smyth told him he would do his best.
"I understand your frustration," he said. "But Artemis Trading has come up in the course of an investigation and we would be derelict in our duties if we didn't follow it up."
"What has Artemis got to do with any investigation?" Gerald asked.
"I'm afraid I can't go into that. Let's just say we received a tip off, and we had to check it out. We've been trying to locate your son. Do you know where Luke is?"
"Why are you looking for Luke?"

"Do you know where he is?"

"Of course I know where he is," Gerald said. "He's my son. He's in Peru."

"Peru?"

"Why are you looking for him?"

"Are you sure he's in Peru?" DI Smyth said.

"Unless there's another Machu Pichu somewhere. He sent me a WhatsApp with a photo of him at Machu Pichu yesterday."

"What's he doing there?" DI Smyth said.

"He's taken a year out to travel. His grades were outstanding, and the university had no problem with him deferring. What's this all about?"

"When did he leave?"

"A week after his final exam," Gerald said. "It will have been early June."

"And he's been out of the country ever since?"

"He has. Will there be anything else? I'm supposed to be in Grimsby right now. We've got a shipment ready to leave and I need to sign it off."

DI Smyth decided to take a chance. "

"Do you know a man by the name of Patrick Carroll?"

"Of course I know him."

"In what capacity are you acquainted?"

"I was the one who was responsible for getting him off the streets for a while."

"I'm not following you," DI Smyth said.

"It was a few years ago. It was my testimony that ensured that he was convicted. Him and two of his heavies."

"What was he convicted of?"

"Some Mickey Mouse thing," Gerald said. "He was behind the murder of a friend of mine. His thugs got life, but Carroll's lawyer made sure he got off with little more than a slap on the wrist. Now, if there's nothing else, I really have to be going. Or do I need to contact my lawyer and let him explain a few things to you?"

"That won't be necessary," DI Smyth said. "I apologise once again for the inconvenience."

* * *

While DI Smyth was eating humble pie, Smith was on the road heading in no particular direction. He needed to think. There was something definitely *off* about the events that had led up to the raid on the offices of Artemis Trading, and he hoped the drive would help to clear his head a bit. Smith had never trusted in coincidence before, and this time was no different. Often when the pieces of an investigation come together so easily it's because somebody wants them to fit. Smith knew that this puzzle was far from complete, and he was furious that the other people on the team couldn't see that.

He slowed down when the lights turned red up ahead and a sign on the side of the road caught his eye. He was heading east on Hull Road and the sign was for Murton Park. The lights changed and Smith indicated to turn left. He joined the A64 and increased his speed. Spots of rain were hitting the windscreen, and the sky had an eerie orange tinge to it.

The industrial estate in Murton wasn't a very big one. Smith counted no more than half a dozen warehouses and Jones' Logistics was easy to find from the massive name on the roof of the warehouse building. He parked in the car park and got out of the car. The rain was coming down harder now. After showing his ID to the security guard at the entrance and explaining the nature of his visit he was buzzed through and given directions to the reception area.

His phone beeped as he walked to tell him he'd received a message. It was from Baldwin. Her contact had managed to pinpoint the rough location of Stacey Watts' phone when the message was sent to her boyfriend. It was by no means a precise location, but it gave Smith something to go on. The signal had been picked up by three cell phone masts. By triangulating the signal, it showed that the phone had been used somewhere between Heworth and Derwenthorpe. Smith remembered that the offices of Artemis Trading were situated almost smack bang in the middle of that area. The bins where Emily Grant had been found were inside the perimeter too. Smith decided he would check out the area after he'd spoken to someone at Jones' Logistics.

"Can I help you, sir?"

The woman's voice made Smith look up from his phone. He showed her his ID.

"I need a list of everybody who works here."

"What is this regarding?"

"I can't discuss that," Smith said. "Look, I don't have a warrant and to be honest, I don't think I'll be able to get one anyway but if you could help me out, I'd really appreciate it."

"I don't think I'm allowed to give out that kind of information."

"Please," Smith said. "Help me out here. It's more to put my mind at ease than anything else. I'm particularly interested in the night shift staff."

The woman remained silent for a while. She chewed her bottom lip and frowned.

"OK," she said eventually. "Follow me."

She led him to a small office and sat down in front of a laptop. She tapped the keypad, and a list of names appeared on the screen.

"Do you need me to print it?"

"That won't be necessary," Smith told her. "Is this everyone who works here."

"Everyone," she confirmed. "From the office staff to the warehouse operatives."

Smith looked carefully at the list of people. He scanned the names and then read it again.

"Are you sure this is everybody who works here?"

"Everybody."

Smith didn't know what the information on the screen was telling him, but he did know one thing for certain: Jack and Steven Norman didn't work for Jones' Logistics. The two brothers who found Emily Grant last night lied to him.

CHAPTER FIFTY TWO

"Has anyone heard from Smith?" DI Smyth asked. "He's not answering his phone."
Whitton, Bridge and the DCs King and Moore were taking a break in the canteen.
"He said he wanted to check something out at City Hospital," Whitton said.
"What exactly is he going to check out?"
"He didn't elaborate."
"If you hear from him again," DI Smyth said. "Tell him to get his backside back here. I will not tolerate another one of his solo crusades."
   "Where do we go from here, sir?" DC King asked.
They were all feeling deflated after the disappointment at the Artemis Trading offices.
"I don't know, Kerry," DI Smyth said. "I really don't know. I don't like admitting it, but it seems the investigation has hit a brick wall and I'm struggling to find a way through it."
   "Smith seems convinced that we're being manipulated," DC King said. "He firmly believes that we're being spoon-fed info to throw us off track, and I'm starting to agree with him."
"As much as I hate to admit it," DI Smyth said. "Smith was right about Artemis Trading. I don't know how he knew it, but he did."
"It's clear that the people behind *The Workshop* are aware of Artemis Trading," Bridge said. "And they seem to know a lot about the people who work there. I don't think it's a coincidence that a bloke called Luke has come up more than once in the investigation and the CEO of the company happens to have a son of the same name."
"I dropped the ball there," DC Moore admitted. "I was so focused on the photos of him and his dad on his Facebook profile I completely overlooked

what was right in front of my face. I checked again, and there were loads of photos of him in South America going back to June. That was a huge blunder on my part."

"Don't dwell on it, Harry," DI Smyth said. "What now?"

His phone started to ring before anyone could answer. A glance at the screen told him it was Smith.

"It's the prodigal son," he said and activated the speakerphone.

"What the hell are you up to?"

"Just doing my job, boss," Smith said.

"Whitton said you were at the hospital."

"I also checked out Jones' Logistics. The brothers who found Emily Grant lied to us – they don't work there. I think they're employed by *The Workshop*."

"That's ridiculous," DI Smyth said. "If that was the case, why would they take Emily to hospital? Why not take her back to *The Workshop*?"

"That's the million-dollar question. And it's one that took me a while to figure out the answer to."

"I'm listening."

"How did the raid on the Artemis Trading offices go?"

"Fuck off."

Everyone turned to look at DI Smyth. Their boss rarely swore.

"Fair enough," Smith said. "I deserved that. I got someone to pull up the CCTV from the car park at the hospital from last night. A very helpful woman not only found footage of the Norman brothers' van, she was also able to print out a decent still shot of the two of them. I showed it to Emily Grant and guess who the younger one is?"

"Steven?" DI Smyth remembered.

"If that's even his real name," Smith said. "It's the same bloke who introduced himself as Luke just before he abducted her."

"Why didn't she recognise him?" DC Moore said.

"When they found her she was out of it," Smith explained. "She was unconscious, so she wouldn't have seen either of their faces."

"It still doesn't explain why they took her to hospital," DI Smyth said. "You haven't answered the million-dollar question."

"Misdirection, boss," Smith said.

"Your favourite word."

"Not really, but that's what this was all about. They've been in complete control here. They're calling the shots, and taking Emily to hospital was all part of a complicated contingency plan."

"You've lost me there," DI Smyth said.

"I was a bit lost myself for a while, but I think we've been the victims of an elaborate double bluff."

"A what?" DC Moore said.

"It's a poker thing," Smith said. "They knew Emily would talk. They knew she would tell us about Luke, and they realised she would probably also be able to describe the place where she was being held captive. Artemis Trading really *is* behind *The Workshop* – they made sure everything pointed in their direction to ensure that we discounted them because nothing can be linked to them."

"You're talking in riddles," Bridge said.

"I think I'm starting to understand what he means," DC King said. "The CEO of Artemis really does have a son called Luke. He just happened to give blood at the same place where Kirsty Davies donated blood."

"I wasn't aware of that part," Smith said.

"We spoke to the CEO earlier," DI Smyth said. "His son happens to have the perfect alibi. He's thousands of miles away in South America."

"There you go then," Smith said. "We dismissed that immediately and turned our focus away from Artemis Trading. They've been dictating the narrative from the very beginning."

"We're going to need that CCTV footage from the hospital," DI Smyth said.

"Already onto it, boss," Smith said. "I asked the lovely lady at the hospital to email it to you. It gives us a partial plate, so we might get lucky."

"You're on form today," DI Smyth said and turned to Whitton. "Did you give him three shredded wheat this morning?"

"Sir?" Whitton said.

"Perhaps it's before your time."

"That's why they pay me the big bucks, boss," Smith said.

"Where are you now?" DI Smyth said. "Are you still at the hospital?"

"There's one more thing I need to check out," Smith said.

"Do I need to remind you that this isn't a one-man team?"

"Of course not. Stacey Watts' boyfriend received a message from her telling him she wasn't coming to his place as planned, but I don't think she was the one who wrote the message. Baldwin got me a rough location of where the phone was when the message was sent."

"How did she manage to do that so quickly?"

"It's probably better that you don't know," Smith said.

"You're not to go there alone," DI Smyth said. "Is that clear?"

"No worries."

"I mean it, Smith. Tell me where you are."

"I'll send you my location," Smith said. "And I want you to arrange for security at the hospital. I've got a sinking feeling that Emily Grant is still in danger."

"What makes you say that?"

"Just a feeling," Smith said. "I think the client has paid up front for the *product*, and the people at *The Workshop* will not want to disappoint the client. Emily is in grave danger."

"I'll arrange for one of the uniforms to stay outside her room if it will make you happy."

"It will," Smith said. "I'll send you my location now."

"Do that. And wait for us to get there before you do anything stupid."

The drone on the other end of the line told him that Smith had already hung up. The phone beeped and DI Smyth swiped the screen. Smith had sent him his location.

CHAPTER FIFTY THREE

Smith decided to start at the bins where Emily Grant had been found. He'd placed his phone on the dashboard with the GPS function activated. He estimated that Emily would probably have only been able to cover half a mile at most in her drugged condition, and he studied the map on his phone. When he'd spoken to her at the hospital, she'd told him she hadn't been able to remember much about the journey she took before she ended up at the bins. It was dark and her mind was foggy from the sedative.

According to the information Baldwin had given him, Stacey Watts' phone had been caught by three of the masts and this gave Smith an area of roughly one square mile to consider. He drove slowly, looking for potential places where *The Workshop* could be as he went. There wasn't much traffic on the roads here and he wondered if the location of the human meat market had been chosen because of this.

He slowed down further when he spotted a cluster of buildings up ahead. When he got closer he saw that they were all in a state of disrepair and none of them looked like they'd been used for a while. Smith pulled up next to the nearest one and got out of the car. He knew he ought to wait for the rest of the team to arrive, but that had never stopped him before, so he made his way to the front of the building.

There was a door at the front that had definitely seen better days. The wood was rotten in places, and it was in dire need of a lick of paint. Two of the panes of glass were broken. Smith turned the handle and, to his surprise the door opened. He went inside and a sound behind him caused him to stop dead. He turned around and saw the white van crawling up the road in the direction of his car. He closed the door and stood, looking through the gap where the glass once was.

The van carried on past his car and stopped in front of one of the buildings further along. Smith watched as two men got out and headed for the building. It was the Norman brothers. They were walking quickly, and they walked with purpose. They knew exactly where they were going. Smith wondered if they'd paid much attention to his car.

He waited until they were inside the house and opened the door. He snapped a couple of photographs of the van's registration number, sent a quick message to DI Smyth and headed towards the house the two brothers had gone inside.

They hadn't locked the door behind them and Smith deduced that they weren't too bothered about the red Ford Sierra parked down the street. Smith pushed open the door and listened carefully. He could make out the sound of voices coming from somewhere inside. He headed in that direction.

The beep of his phone sounded like the peal of church bells in Smith's ears, and he cursed himself for not turning the phone to silent. He switched the ringtone off and hoped he wasn't too late. The message was from DI Smyth informing him that they were on their way. The muffled voices continued, and he carried on walking. There was a strange smell inside the house – it was a mixture of sweat and something sweet. Smith was sure he'd come across the floral scent before.

The first door he tried was locked. The voices had stopped, but there was another noise now – it sounded like something being scraped across the floor. Smith could feel his muscles tensing on their own and he sensed that something was about to happen.

He wasn't wrong. The locked door opened behind him, and he felt an arm around his neck. A figure emerged from further along the corridor and raced towards him. Smith couldn't tell if it was a man or a woman – they were wearing a facemask and a pair of strange goggles.

He dug his nails into the arm that was choking him, and he turned to face his assailant. It was the younger of the Norman brothers, Steven. "You're in the wrong place," Steven said in a voice not much louder than a whisper.
The other person had removed the mask and goggles now and Smith saw that it was Steven's brother Jack.

"Stick him with the needle," Steven said.
Jack raised the syringe in the air and, at the same time Steven made another attempt to restrain Smith by wrapping his arm around his neck. Smith ducked just in time, turned around and spat as much saliva into Steven's eyes as he could manage. The accuracy wasn't great, but it seemed to have the desired effect. Steven instantly raised both hands to his eyes.
"Fuck me," Smith said. "That actually does work."

He turned his attention to Jack. The needle of the syringe was dangerously close so Smith did the only thing he could think of. With all the strength he could manage he raised his leg and kicked Jack hard in the balls. This proved to be even more effective than a glob of spit to the eyes and Jack went down, dropping the syringe in the process. Smith kicked him once more in the head for good measure and reached down for the syringe.

He jabbed Jack hard in the arm and pressed the plunger.
"I reckon he's going to need that," he said to Steven.
He was talking to himself. Jack's brother had gone. Smith turned to see the open door and soon afterwards the sound of an engine starting up could be heard. Smith raced outside and saw the van speeding off down the road.
"Fuck it."
The rest of the team still hadn't arrived.

Smith went back inside the house and a quick glance at Jack Norman told him he was lights out. Smith carried on down the corridor and stopped at a door at the end. What he found on the other side of the door wasn't what he was expecting at all. It was a reception area. There was a large desk, and a few chairs dotted around. The walls were covered with pictures of luxury vehicles. There was one door at the back of the room and later the forensics team who would arrive to examine the premises would find a broken key jammed inside the lock.

On the left was another door. Smith opened it and gasped. Two women were huddled in the corner of the room, close together. Next to them was a bed with someone on it.

"Stay where you are," Smith told the women.

Neither of them spoke.

"What kind of monsters are you?"

Nothing.

Smith leaned over the woman on the bed. He checked her pulse to find a weak throb. She was still alive. She opened her eyes and looked right at Smith.

"Kirsty?" he said.

Her eyes widened and she nodded.

CHAPTER FIFTY FOUR

"She's going to be fine," DI Smyth said.
He and Smith were at City Hospital. Kirsty Davies had been taken there and instantly given a blood transfusion. She was still very weak, but she was stable, and the doctors told them that she should make a full recovery.

Jack Norman was in the same hospital. He was sleeping the sleep of the dead in a private room, with only a uniformed officer for company. The van his brother had been in was picked up shortly after he left the premises of *The Workshop*, and he was now enjoying the finest hospitality York Police had to offer.

The two women Smith found in the house were also in custody, but neither of them had spoken a word since their arrest. Inside the house they'd found what they were looking for. Surgical saws, bone saws, and an array of other surgical tools had been discovered along with enough sedative to knock out an army. Smith had found *The Workshop*.

"Do we have any news from Grimsby?" he asked.
"Not yet," DI Smyth said. "We're liaising with the local police there, as well as Customs and Excise and they've promised to let us know as soon as they find anything."
"What about Gerald Nelson?"

They now believed that the CEO of Artemis Trading was in such a hurry to get to the port to ensure that the shipment of luxury vehicles left without issue. Smith was convinced they would find something inside those cars that could be linked to *The Workshop*.

"We'll be the first to know if anything happens," DI Smyth said.

"I'm going outside to smoke a cigarette," Smith said.
"I think I'll join you," DI Smyth said.

"You don't smoke."

"I used to," DI Smyth said. "And a cigarette is just what the doctor ordered right now. If you'll excuse the pun."

"Pun?"

DI Smyth raised an eyebrow. "Doctor? Hospital?"

"I think I need some sleep," Smith said.

They were halfway to the exit when a woman approached. It was Emily Grant.

"I heard about Kirsty," she said.

"Shouldn't you be in bed?" Smith said.

"I've been given permission to go and see her. But I wanted to thank you."

"What for?"

"For saving her life. I believe you were the one who found her."

"You should be thanking yourself," Smith told her. "You were the one who saved her life. And I actually wanted to thank you for something else – that thing where you spit into someone's eyes really does work."

Emily laughed. Her blue eye seemed much brighter than Smith remembered.

"What now, boss?" Smith asked outside.

"We've still got a long road ahead of us," DI Smyth said.

He took a long drag of the cigarette and coughed.

"I wonder how many more of them we're going to find," Smith said. "Victims of *The Workshop* I mean."

"The main thing is it's over," DI Smyth said.

"Is it though? Whenever you have sickos with big enough bank balances, you're always going to have someone who'll be there to fulfil their depraved wishes. I'm not sure I want to do this job anymore."

"You don't mean that."

"Don't I? What kind of a world do we live in where human beings are being traded like pieces of meat?"

"A world where people like you and I are paid to put a stop to it."

"When are we going to hear back from Grimsby?" Smith asked.

"As soon as they know anything, we'll be informed. Oh, before I forget, I thought you might want to see this."

He reached inside his jacket, took out a sheet of paper and handed it to Smith.

"What's this?" Smith said.

"Read it."

Smith unfolded it and started to read.

"You're kidding me. Where did you get that?"

"I asked PC Miller to make me a copy of the accident report he filed."

"But this could get him into serious shit," Smith said. "He's put it on file that it was him who reversed into my car."

"I believe you owe PC Miller a drink or two. What's done is done, and since that report states the vehicle he reversed into was stationary there will be no need to delve into the insurance lapse."

"Can I keep this?" Smith said.

"As long as you don't tell anyone else about it."

Smith finished his cigarette and lit another.

"What happened to the German?"

"What?" DI Smyth said.

"Emily Grant spoke about a man with a German accent. What happened to him?"

* * *

"There's something blocking the door," Billie Jones said.
She gave it a shove, but the door still wouldn't budge. After trying the handle, she realised the door wasn't locked when it opened a couple of inches.

"Do you smell that?" Billie asked.

"Smells like perfume," Webber said. "It's very familiar."

"Help me to try and push the door open. There's definitely something behind it.

Webber gave the door a hard shove with his shoulder and the gap widened. Together, he and Billie managed to push it further open and soon there was a large enough space for Billie to get inside to see what was behind it.

"We need an ambulance now," she called out a moment later. "It's a woman. She's unconscious – her pulse is very weak, but she's still alive."

CHAPTER FIFTY FIVE

Smith opened the door to his house and went inside. Lucy had called him and told him he needed to come home because of some kind of family emergency. DI Smyth had told him to go. Gerald Nelson still hadn't been located. The CEO of Artemis Trading was proving to be a difficult man to track down, but DI Smyth was confident that it was only a matter of time before he was found. He promised to let Smith know the moment that happened.

Lucy was sitting in the living room with Laura and Fran. Both girls looked like they'd been caught doing something they shouldn't have been doing, and Smith wondered what was going on. He asked Lucy as much.

"Tell him." She said to the girls.

Neither Laura nor Fran spoke.

"I haven't got time for games," Smith said. "Laura, what have you done?"

She remained silent.

"I really don't have time for this," Smith said. "We've reached a crucial stage in the investigation, and I'm needed back at work."

"You're always needed at work," Laura said.

"It's my job," Smith said.

"And it's a very important one," Lucy added.

"It's more important than me," Laura said. "And Fran."

Smith wasn't expecting this.

"What's brought this on?"

"You're always busy at work," Laura said. "You don't even notice us anymore."

"Of course I notice you," Smith said.

"You went away on holiday without us." Fran had found her voice.

"What?" It was all Smith could think of to say.

"We want to live with Lucy and Darren," Laura said. "At least they care about us."

"I'm really not in the mood for a couple of spoilt brats," Smith said. "You're eight years old, and it's time you learned how things work for eight-year-olds in the real world."

"But..." Laura began.

"But nothing," Smith cut her short. "In my day, kids had respect. I don't give a fuck what the namby pamby do-gooders tell the kids these days – in this house you're the child and I'm the adult, and that means you do not get a say in how things work. Have you got that? Anyway, I thought you were both sick."

The silence that followed seemed to last forever.

Lucy was the one to break it.

"Neither of them is really sick," she said. "They saw a thing on the Internet that shows people how to make it look like you've got a fever."

"What?" Smith looked at Laura. "Is that true?"

"It's not hard," Laura said.

"Why?" Smith said. "Why would you do that? Is there something bothering you at school? Is that why you made it look like you were ill? So you didn't have to face whatever it is at school that's bothering you?"

"You don't care."

"Of course I care. Wait, are you telling me you did this for attention?"

"It didn't work though."

Smith's phone started to ring and for once, he debated whether to ignore it. A quick glance at the screen told him that wasn't an option.

"I have to take this."

Laura didn't comment on this. She and Fran both fixed him with icy glares and left the room. Smith could hear their footsteps as they tramped upstairs.

He answered the call.

"Boss."

It was DI Smyth.

"Gerald Nelson has been found," he said.

"Where is he?" Smith asked.

"On his way back to York," DI Smyth said. "In the back of a police car. We've had a development at the scene of *The Workshop* too. Webber and Billie found a woman in a storeroom there. She was barely alive, and she's been taken to hospital."

"Do you think she's another victim?"

"It doesn't appear so. It looks like she panicked when the troops arrived and injected herself with what she believed to be a lethal dose of tranquilizer. She miscalculated and she's probably going to survive. There's more – you've met her."

"Who is she?" Smith asked.

"She's Emily Grant's mother."

"You can't be serious?"

"I'm afraid I am. It's Hilda Lewis, and she's got a lot of explaining to do when she wakes up."

* * *

There were so many thoughts racing through Smith's head as he drove back to the station that he almost ran a red light and collided with a bus. It was a close call, and the driver of the bus offered an opinion or two with a few choice words out of the window, but luckily nobody was hurt.

Smith couldn't stop thinking about Laura and Fran. He couldn't believe that two eight-year-old girls could think up something like that. He'd never known Laura to behave in a devious manner before and he wondered if it was something to be concerned about. He decided that he would discuss it with Whitton later.

Equally concerning was Hilda Lewis's presence at *The Workshop*. What was the mother of a potential victim doing there? Was it possible that Hilda played a part in her daughter's abduction? If that was the case, then the world was even more depraved than Smith originally thought. It really was sickening to believe a mother could do something like that.

He wondered if they were going to get anything out of Gerald Nelson. It was looking likely that the Artemis Trading CEO was behind *The Workshop*, but Smith didn't hold out much hope of him making life easy for them. He had a sinking feeling that they were going to have to get the information they needed the hard way.

He parked his car in the car park at the station and smoked a quick cigarette. He needed to make some sort of sense out of the events of the past twenty-four hours. He knew that this was far from over. *The Workshop* had been found, and operations had been suspended for the time being, but Smith didn't believe that this was the end of it. There was far too much at stake for the people involved, and he wouldn't be surprised if another of their contingency plans would catch them all by surprise. He stubbed out the cigarette and headed inside the station.

CHAPTER FIFTY SIX

The rest of the team had been busy in Smith's absence. When he came inside the small conference room, Whitton, Bridge and the DCs King and Moore didn't even acknowledge him. All of them were focused on their individual tasks. Smith walked over to Whitton and placed a hand on her shoulder.

"We need to have a chat about the girls later."

She looked up from her work. "What's happened?"

"Nothing we can't figure out. What are you looking at?"

"According to the Deeds Office," Whitton said. "Artemis Trading owns all of the properties in that row of buildings where the *Workshop* was located."

"Why would they want to own a bunch of derelict buildings?" Smith said. "Surely the board of directors would want to know the reason for it."

"Harry seems to think the sale of the properties probably fell under the radar," Whitton said. "The purchase price for the whole row was minimal – small fry for a company of their size."

"It's not uncommon," DC Moore joined in. "A large conglomerate purchases land under the guise of future development possibilities. The whole lot was bought just over a year ago for little more than the cost of a few luxury vehicles."

The conversation was cut short when DI Smyth came inside the room. He looked haggard, and Smith reckoned he didn't look much better himself.

"Problems, boss?" he said.

"You could say that," DI Smyth said. "Gerald Nelson has arrived. He's been booked in and he's refusing to say a word until he's spoken to his legal team."

"We expected as much. Where is he?"

"In one of the holding cells."

"Let him stew," Smith said. "How long are we talking before his lawyer gets here?"

"A few hours at least."

"Do we have any news from Grimsby?" Smith asked.

"Not yet. The Artemis shipment was due to leave today, but the entire container has been seized, and Customs are busy sifting through it now."

"They're going to find something," Smith decided. "Why else would Nelson be in such a hurry to leave earlier?"

He rubbed his eyes and stretched his arms. "You spoke to the man, didn't you?"

"We had a brief chat after the botched raid at the offices," DI Smyth said.

"What did he look like?"

"What?"

"Never mind," Smith said.

He stretched his arms again and left the room.

The duty sergeant looked even more harassed than DI Smyth, and Smith deduced that he'd been given a hard time by Gerald Nelson.

"Where is he?" Smith asked.

"Cell number three. He's not a happy chap."

"I don't imagine he is. I just need a moment with him."

"You shouldn't really be talking to him without his lawyer present."

"No worries," Smith said. "I'm not actually here to speak to him."

He headed straight for the holding cells. A figure was sleeping in the first one. Smith didn't disturb him. Gerald Nelson was sitting on the bed in number 3. He had his hands over his face. Smith took out his phone.

"Say cheese."

Gerald looked up at him. "What?"

Smith took a number of photographs of him in quick succession.

"What the hell are you doing?"

"Get some rest," Smith told him. "We'll speak soon."

Whitton wasn't in the small conference room when he returned. Bridge told him she was taking a breather in the canteen. Smith's phone started to ring when he was on his way there. The screen told him it was a number not in his contacts so he let it ring out.

Whitton was sitting at the table by the window. Smith joined her.

"What was that about earlier?" she said. "You were all cryptic about Gerald Nelson's appearance and then you just left."

"I think the CEO of Artemis Trading is the mystery German," Smith said. "Emily Grant talked about a bloke with a German accent, and I think it's Nelson. And if that's the case there will be traces of him at the *Workshop*."

"What difference does it make?" Whitton said. "We already know he's involved – he's the CEO of a company that is involved beyond a shadow of a doubt."

"That's irrelevant," Smith said. "And I know for a fact that his legal team will say the same thing."

"We've got enough on him to hold him," Whitton said. "All we need to do now is follow the paper trail right back to when this started."

"That's precisely what we do not want to do. I could be wrong, but I bet that Nelson has a contingency plan in place that will show that his hands are clean in this. His lawyers will claim that he was simply the man at the helm of a company that was used as a front for something truly sinister, and he had no idea it was going on. He'll be embarrassed beyond belief – he'll probably be forced to resign but eventually he'll be a free man. I want something more concrete than a trail of paper."

"How are you going to get that?" Whitton said. "For all we know, he'll have made sure not to leave any forensic evidence of his time at the *Workshop*."

"If that's the case," Smith said. "So be it, but we have something better than that."

"What?"

"Witness statements," Smith said. "Both Kirsty Davies and Emily Grant have seen his face. If they can confirm that the missing German is in fact, Gerald Nelson, we'll have the fucker backed into a corner no fancy legal team will be able to get him out of."

CHAPTER FIFTY SEVEN

"The news from Grimsby is dire."
DI Smyth had called the team together to discuss the new developments. Smith and Whitton had just returned from the hospital. Emily Grant had confirmed that Gerald Nelson was indeed the mystery German. Smith knew that it would probably be enough to ensure that the CEO of Artemis Trading spent the rest of his life behind bars.

"According to the spokesperson from Customs and Excise I spoke to," DI Smyth continued. "None of the officers had seen anything like it before. Some of them have decades of experience under their belts and they were sickened beyond belief. The unfortunate officials who have been tasked with drawing up an inventory of the items in the shipment will probably need counselling afterwards."

"The body parts were hidden in the cars, weren't they?" Smith said.

"They were," DI Smyth confirmed. "And it is highly likely they would have been delivered to the clients without incident if we hadn't got there in time. Once the container vessels leave British waters it becomes a jurisdictional nightmare."

"What did they find?" Smith asked the question on everybody's mind.

"It's going to take a long time to confirm where the body parts came from," DI Smyth said. "But I think we can safely assume they will be tied to the bodies we've recently recovered. And there's a rather disturbing aspect to the raid on the luxury vehicle shipment."

"There were more body parts than we thought, weren't there?" Smith said.

DI Smyth nodded his head. "Customs recovered the head, arms and legs that were probably once attached to Zoe Granger's body. There were also bags and bags of organs packed in ice boxes. In another vehicle were the hands and feet of Stacey Watts. There were six fingers and six toes on each limb, and numerous bags of human blood were also recovered. This is just the tip of the iceberg."

Smith's ringtone sounded and the screen told him it was the same number that had appeared earlier. He switched the phone off.

"What about the clients?" DC King brought up. "Is there any way to make them accountable?"

"I don't think there is, Kerry," DI Smyth said.

"But they should pay for their involvement in this," DC King said. "They can't get away with it."

"They'll be seriously out of pocket," Smith said. "They will have definitely paid up front, and they're not going to receive the products they ordered. And that's going to piss them off."

"They're hardly likely to take it further though, are they?" DC Moore said. "It's not like they can go to trading standards with something like this."

"No," Smith said. "But they will find a way to get even. These kind of people are not people who will take this lying down."

"What now?" Bridge wondered. "Is it finally over?"

"We still have a lot of follow-up work to get through," DI Smyth said. "But the main thing is the *Workshop* has been shut down, and the clients of these sick bastards are now well aware that this kind of barbarism will not be tolerated in this day and age."

The door to the room opened and Baldwin came in.

"Sorry to interrupt," she said. "But Gerald Nelson's lawyer has arrived."

Smith was on his feet in an instant.

"I wouldn't get too excited, Sarge," Baldwin said. "From what I can gather, his lawyer is advising him to go the *no comment* route."

Smith shrugged his shoulders. "I'm not interested in anything he has to say anyway. He's not legally obliged to tell us anything, but he is legally obliged to sit in an interview room and listen to what I have to tell him."

* * *

Gerald Nelson's body language told Smith that this was going to be more satisfying than he anticipated. The arrogant CEO was sitting upright in the chair in the interview room with his arms folded across his chest. Smith thought the expression on his face was one of mild amusement. This wasn't a man who expected to be charged with his involvement in multiple murders.

DI Smyth went through the motions for the record and Gerald's lawyer was the first to speak.

"I have advised my client not to answer any of your questions."

He was a tall, stick-like man with a glass eye. He'd introduced himself as Barton Plover and Smith had taken an instant dislike to him.

"So," he added. "If you could say what you have to say, as quickly as possible, we can move on to the next stage in this farce."

Smith nodded. "No worries. Gerald – is it OK if I call you Gerald?"

"No comment."

"I'll take that as a yes then. Gerald, how on earth did you get involved in something like this?"

"No…"

"I'll stop you there, if that's alright," Smith said. "We all know you're not interested in talking, so I'll save you the hassle. We know you were the main man at *The Workshop*. We know that you used the company you head up as a front to get the depraved products to the clients. That's not what we're here to discuss. The evidence of that cannot be disputed. We also know that you took an active role in the day-to-day operations at *The Workshop*. We have two witnesses who can put you there."

If Smith expected to see a reaction to this, he didn't get one. Gerald Nelson remained unfazed. He whispered something in Barton Plover's ear.

"Could you please repeat that for the tape?" DI Smyth said.

"My client was merely voicing his concerns about your so-called witnesses," Barton said.

"Both of them can put your client at *The Workshop*," Smith told him.

"I see. And do you have any other evidence to prove that Mr Nelson was ever there? Perhaps something more tangible than a couple of women who I believe were rather traumatised at the time. Two women with enough sedative in their systems to knock out an army hardly make for reliable witnesses, wouldn't you agree?"

Smith didn't know if Forensics had found anything to place Gerald Nelson there, but he wasn't particularly troubled about it.

"Is there anything else you'd like to bring up?" Barton said. "My client is an innocent man who was caught up in something heinous, not by choice. He deeply regrets the circumstances that will no doubt have severe repercussions for the company he was entrusted to lead, and he will be tendering his resignation after a discussion with the board. A statement will be released as soon as that discussion is concluded."

"Something heinous?" Smith said. "Your client was responsible for acts of brutality none of the people in my team has ever come across before. None of us ever imagined someone could sink to such depths of depravity. Hardened customs officials were sickened by what they found in the vehicles your client was so keen to get shipped off."

"As I pointed out," Barton said.

"I'm not finished talking," Smith said. "Your client knows what he did. Whether he gets away with it or not doesn't change that fact. He knows what he did, and the people who paid serious money for the sick products he promised them also know what he did."

He stopped there and looked straight at Gerald.

"Perhaps you failed to consider that."

Gerald's expression changed. It was a subtle change, but Smith noticed it.

"Don't underestimate the reach of these people, Gerald."

"I fail to see the relevance of this," Barton commented.

"The relevance is this," Smith said. "Whether your client is acquitted or whether he gets sent down for life, the outcome is still going to be the same."

He suddenly remembered something Patrick Carroll had said. It was a term he wasn't particularly fond of, but it seemed somewhat appropriate now.

"You're a dead man walking, Gerald. You and your cohorts in *The Workshop*. You've ripped off some very nasty people, and they're not going to take too kindly to that."

"This is unacceptable," Barton said.

"They'll find you wherever you go." Smith wasn't quite finished yet. "You're a dead man walking."

"I suggest we wrap things up there," DI Smyth said.

"I couldn't agree more," Smith said.

CHAPTER FIFTY EIGHT

"Gerald Nelson is dead."

DI Smyth hadn't even bothered to say hello when he phoned.

"What happened?" Smith said.

"He was found in his cell at Full Sutton," DI Smyth said. "Multiple stab wounds. There'll be a full enquiry, but nobody is going to talk."

Gerald had made a full confession. The ex-CEO of Artemis Trading had told them everything. Smith wondered if he thought he would be safer locked up in prison than out on the streets, but if that was the case he'd vastly underestimated the reach of the people he'd chosen as clients. Gerald had been sent to Full Sutton while he awaited the trial. He'd been judged and sentenced long before the justice system had its chance to dole out punishment. Smith knew that it was only a matter of time before the other people involved in *The Workshop* met the same end.

Jack and Steven Norman were also enjoying the hospitality of Full Sutton Prison. The evidence against the two brothers was compelling and there was little doubt they would spend the rest of their lives behind bars. Smith wondered how long it would take for the clients of *The Workshop* to catch up with them too.

The two women found at *The Workshop* had spoken at length about their involvement. Both were illegal immigrants and both of them had been threatened with their lives if they didn't comply. Smith wasn't entirely certain what was going to happen to them.

Hilda Lewis's motive was the most difficult to comprehend. Emily Grant's mother had been willing to sacrifice the life of a daughter for a few pieces of silver. Smith hadn't been involved in her interview. He'd refused outright – he wasn't sure if he would be able to control himself, but Bridge and DC Moore had told him it was the hardest interview they'd ever had to conduct.

Hilda and Colin were destitute. They'd stacked up huge debts and they'd seen no other way out. The whole thing made Smith feel sick to the stomach and he would lose no sleep if it later came out that they'd gone the same way as Gerald Nelson.

"Are you still there?" DI Smyth said.

"Still here," Smith confirmed.

"Rumour has it that Artemis Trading is finished."

"It's hardly surprising," Smith said. "Something like this is pretty hard to come back from. I couldn't give a fuck to be honest."

"A lot of innocent people lost a lot of money when the share price plummeted."

"Once again," Smith said. "Tell someone who gives a fuck. Will there be anything else? We promised the girls we'd take them to the seaside. We've been neglecting them recently, and they're really looking forward to it."

"You do know it's going to rain."

"Then we'll get wet," Smith said. "I'll see you in a couple of days."

His phone started to ring as soon as he'd ended the call. It was a number not in his contact list.

He answered it anyway.

"You're a hard man to get hold of. I've been trying you for days."

Smith recognised the voice immediately – it was Horace Nagel.

"It's been a busy time," Smith said.

"So I believe. Did you get the outcome you wanted?"

"I reckon we got the best outcome we could have hoped for. I suppose I should thank you for your part in that."

"I did what I could."

"There's one thing I still don't understand," Smith said. "Why go about it in such a roundabout way?"

"I don't think I understand."

"You knew all about *The Workshop*," Smith said. "Why be so cryptic with the information? You could have just come out with it."

"You know why," Horace said. "How many times do I have to tell you – I'm not a snitch."

"Fair enough."

"It all worked out in the end."

"Not really," Smith said. "There's still the matter of the carjacking thing we need to discuss. We need to have a talk about that."

"Talk away," Horace said.

Smith began, but the drone on the other end of the line told him it was a one-sided conversation.

He held the phone up and smiled at it. He couldn't help it. Darren Lewis came into the kitchen.

"What's so funny?"

"You wouldn't get it," Smith said. "Is everybody ready?"

"They're ready," Darren said. "Are you sure you don't want me to drive?"

"I don't think so."

"I still can't believe we got away with the bumper bash with the police car."

"It pays to have friends in high places," Smith said.

"I thought you were totally against the abuse of power. You've always been so anti it in the past."

"Most of the time I am," Smith said. "But sometimes you just think, fuck it – if you can't beat 'em, join 'em."

THE END

Printed in Great Britain
by Amazon